D1245456

TAGO

Appointed regulator in the silver-mining town of Tago, Hart had his work cut out—there was Crazy John Carter, cold-blooded murderer of two kids, who tried to burn Hart alive . . . Then there was silver thief Jake Henry . . . Dan Waterford, out to blow the brains out of the punk who had killed his brother . . . and scheming Lacey, whose last wish was to see a big red hole in Hart's head . . .

JOHN B. HARVEY

TAGO

Complete and Unabridged

LINFORD
Leicester

First published in Great Britain in 1980 by
Pan Books Ltd.,
London

First Linford Edition
published December 1986
by arrangement with
Pan Books Ltd.,
London

British Library CIP Data

Harvey, John, *1938–*
[Tago] Hart: Tago.—Large print ed.—
Linford western library
I. [Tago] II. Title
823′.914[F] PR6058.A698/

ISBN 0-7089-6290-4

Published by
F. A. Thorpe (Publishing) Ltd.
Anstey, Leicestershire
Set by Rowland Phototypesetting Ltd.
Bury St. Edmunds, Suffolk
Printed and bound in Great Britain by
T. J. Press (Padstow) Ltd., Padstow, Cornwall

this is for
Bonney, Kevin and Big Dave:
the Gang of Three

1

THE gunbelt hung from the foot of the bed. It had been looped over the ornamented brass post and then buckled. The belt itself was of strong, dark leather; the buckle square, a less yellow brass than the bed. The gun sat snug in the holster, a Colt Peacemaker .45 with a mother-of-pearl grip. Carved on to the grip were the figures of an eagle and a snake. The eagle, wings out, perched on the body of a snake, as on a branch, its talons gripped tight. The bird's powerful head was turned sideways, its curved beak biting down into the snake's neck. Above that head, the snake twisted sideways, mouth open, fangs drawn but useless. If snakes screamed with fear, with anger, with the coming of death, then that snake would have screamed.

But the scream which cut through the room was human and it was not a sign of pain, hardly of pain at all. The girl threw her arm back so that it hit the thin rail of the bedhead and then the plaster wall behind. She twisted her head to one side, then the other. Her hips thrust forwards and up and when she moved her head again and bit down into the soft flesh at the top of his shoulder it was the man who cried out.

He shook her free and raised himself up with his right arm, straightening it from the elbow. He saw her face and knew that the time had almost come. He closed his eyes as he sank back down and her legs spread wider and caught him tight and hard, at the final moment calling a name that was not his.

They lay there and after a while he rolled off her and on to his side, quietening his breathing. The girl reached out her hand cautiously towards him, as if he might knock it away. He didn't. She traced a line down his chest with her middle finger, pushing it through the curls of dark hair, making small circles. He lay there, listening to the horses passing up and down the street outside, occasionally a wagon. Men's voices drifted up to the first-floor room, becoming louder and harsher. Soon they would be drunken voices and there would be punches being thrown, threats and maybe shooting. But that was later.

For now it was getting dark and the lines in the room were becoming less distinct. His pants were hanging from the back of a chair, dark brown that now looked black. A blue shirt was thrown down on the floor, a light leather vest close by it. Underneath the window were his boots; scuffed, plain leather, one of them folding forwards as it stood there. Inside the other, the right one, it was just possible to pick out the tip of the hilt of the knife he carried there. Well honed and double-bladed, it was usually with him, either inside the boot or hanging from his saddle horn inside its Apache sheath.

"What you thinking?"

He turned towards her: "Nothin'."

"You're awful quiet."

"Yeah."

"Then you must be thinkin'."

He closed his eyes for a second then swung his legs off the bed; the mattress had slipped sideways and his thighs rested on the edge of the iron frame.

"Look . . ." She touched his back with the flat of her hand and it was warm to him. "You ain't mad at me, are you?"

He stood up. "No."

She looked at him with earnest eyes. "I mean on account of . . . when I . . . when . . . I called someone else's name."

She looked away, down at the rumpled sheet.

"It don't matter."

He started to get dressed, not hurrying, looking from time to time through the window. The lights of the saloon down the street were beginning to stand out more clearly. Soon it would be possible to see the stars in the night sky; the moon glowed dully like a shadow of itself.

Hart unbuckled his gunbelt and set it round his body, the leather resting on his hips. Automatically he slid the Colt .45

from the greased holster and spun the chamber, enjoying the purring roll of sound and the exactly balanced weight in his hand. He let the gun fall back and turned towards the bed.

"Be seein' you, maybe."

She looked at him with small, dark eyes. A small pile of coins was stacked on the round table alongside the head of her bed.

"'Bye."

Hart closed the door on her voice. The stairway was lit with a paraffin lamp fixed to a polished brass bracket; other, similar, lights lined both sides of the room below. Upholstered easy chairs and settees, rosewood tables and clean cuspidors. There was a small bar in one corner, a Negro wearing a striped apron standing behind it polishing a glass with a linen cloth. Several girls sat around the room, coloured robes over their underthings, blues and pinks and fern green. A couple of men sat together, smoking cigars and eyeing the women and talking about them in hushed tones.

When Hart reached the foot of the stairs and began to walk towards the door a voice stopped him and made him look over his shoulder.

"You're not going without saying good-bye, Wes?"

The tone was half-mocking, half-scolding; the speaker tall, her black hair swept back about her fine head and held by a clip which sparkled in the orange-yellow light. She was wearing a long gown with a trim of fur at the bottom which swept along the polished wood floor as she walked. The dark blue of the gown contrasted with the soft white skin of her breasts as they showed at the deep fall of the bodice.

"Kate."

She laid a gloved hand upon his arm. "Surely you'll buy a lady a drink first?" her dark eyes smiled at him, teasingly.

"Sure, why not?"

Kate Stein glanced over at the bartender and signalled with her left hand. She and Hart went over to a side booth and sat facing one another.

"Have a good time?"

"Sure."

"Evie's a nice girl."

"Uh-huh." Hart drank some whisky and leaned back, looking at her, aware of the expensive perfume she was wearing.

Kate toyed with her glass. "It's been good since you've been around, Wes." She glanced at him. "Someone to talk to . . . to depend on."

He set down his glass harder than was necessary. "Kate, don't play with me. You don't depend on anyone an' you know it, least of all no man."

"Wes." Her hand reached for him but he shifted his arm clear.

"I bought you a drink, what more d'you want?"

She set her head back and looked at him, staring at the high cheekbones in his lean face, at the stubble around his jaw, the brown hair that fell past his ears and folded over against his shirt collar—at the faded blue of his eyes. He was, Kate would have admitted if forced to it, a handsome man.

"Just a few minutes talk, Wes, that's all."

He nodded and finished his whisky. "That's it, then."

He was standing by the side of the booth when Kate leaned towards him. "One thing, Wes."

"Yeah?"

"Some men are in town, asking for you."

A nerve began ticking at the side of Hart's temple, the familiar hollow rolled over inside his stomach; his eyes narrowed to little more than slits.

"What men?"

"I don't know. They rode in half an hour back. Three of them. Tied up their mounts outside the saloon and began asking for you right off. Charlie, there, he was over there when they come in. Told me soon as he got back."

Hart glanced at the bartender and nodded. "Thanks, Kate. I'll talk to him on the way out."

Half a dozen paces into the room, she called after him: "Take care, Wes."

Hart barely hesitated, carrying on until he came to the bar. Charlie was a light-toned Negro who'd been working for Kate since she'd brought her girls up the Mississippi half a dozen years before. Most of the girls had changed since then—they'd caught a dose of the clap, made a mess of themselves trying to handle their own abortion; they'd got married or simply got too old and tired-looking to do the work any longer—but Charlie was still there.

He smoothed his fine-skinned hands down the sides of his apron and looked at Hart. "Yes, sir?"

"Kate says there's some men lookin' for me. Says you seen 'em."

Charlie nodded. "That's right. Over at the saloon. Come in askin' for you straight off. Sort of loud about it. Let folk know that if they found you they should tell you to get to the saloon an' talk to 'em."

"What sort of men are they, Charlie?"

The Negro took a half pace back and

looked at Hart carefully "Sort of like yourself, I'd say. 'Cept . . ."

"'Cept what?"

"They didn't look so dangerous. Not to me, anyhow."

"Thanks, Charlie."

Hart moved to the door and turned the brass handle. He glanced over his shoulder towards the booths, but Kate Stein was no longer to be seen. He closed the door behind him and stepped into the dark street.

Music spilled from the saloon, a jumble of notes from a piano that needed tuning and a banjo that lacked a musician with more fingers than thumbs. Light hit the boardwalk in leaning rectangles of yellow. Hart stood close by the nearest window and looked in.

The bar ran most of the way down the right-hand side of the room, long and high with a mirror that covered the wall for half of that length. An artist had painted a naked woman on to the mirror, stretched out on a chaise-longue with feathers in her hair. The painting was mostly thin, black outline with occasional features picked out in colour. Below the two red splodges of her breasts two barmen stood talking to one another, ignoring the calls of several customers to be served. From where he was standing, Hart could see the butt of the sawn-off he knew they kept stashed amongst the bottles beneath the bar.

Hart looked over the crowd, pretty big for what was still early in the evening. A line by the bar and then three-quarters of the tables were occupied. There was a game of poker going on near the rear of the room and a couple of men playing blackjack in the furthest corner. A few girls were scattered here and there, but mostly it was the usual mixture of cowhands and miners and men who didn't know where the price of their next drink was coming from.

The piano player had his head bent over the keys, a bald spot on top reflecting under the light above him. He was just starting up a slow Irish ballad with lots of trills that sounded strange on account of the notes that were missing or stuck down. The banjo man sat cradling the base of his instrument into his stomach, no longer playing along but watching.

The three men Hart was interested in were midway between the bar and the piano. One had his back to the window, but the other two were faced towards the front of the room.

Hart didn't recognize either of them, but they seemed familiar enough. Their faces were hard and humourless, eyes mean and narrow. When they spoke to one another it was in short harsh sentences, spitting the words from their mouths. The man on the right had a nose like the back of an axe blade, dark curly hair and a black hat pushed well back on to his head. The one to his side was round-faced, stubbly, his hat hanging down on to his back from a cord about his neck. Both wore rough wool shirts under dark vests, while the third man had on a black broadcloth coat that fitted tightly across his broad shoulders.

Hart couldn't see any of their weapons but he didn't doubt they were there. He left the window and pushed one side of the batwing doors open and walked in quietly. Hardly anyone turned round.

Hart threaded his way to the bar and set one hand flat upon the stained surface.

"Whisky."

The shorter and fatter of the two barmen came towards him, lifting an opened bottle from the shelf beneath the mirror. Beyond the bartender's head Hart could see the three in the middle of the room. He didn't think they'd picked him out yet.

"There's three fellers here wantin' . . ." the barman began.

Hart nodded. "I know. I see 'em."

He tipped a dollar on to the counter and watched as the podgy fingers fumbled his change from a broad pocket at the front of the apron.

"You know who they are?" Hart asked.

The round face moved from side to side. "No. Never seen 'em here before. They wasn't sayin' either."

"Okay."

As Hart lifted back his head to drink the whisky, he noticed the man with the hatchet face lean towards the one with the broadcloth coat and nod his head in the direction of where Hart was standing. Through the mirror Hart watched the man turn slowly round. He saw the high forehead, the pock-marked cheeks and the thin, wide line of the mouth; the suggestion of a cast in the left eye.

Crazy John Carter.

Ten years ago, it had to be, maybe more. Hart had been working as a deputy in a place name of Bandera, down south in Texas. Crazy John had been working as ramrod for one of the spreads close by. Every once in a while he'd ride into town and set about getting as drunk as he could without falling off his feet and throwing up all over himself. Though Hart had seen him do both of those, too.

Just like he'd seen him do other things . . .

Hart threw back the rest of the whisky and turned fast, his right hand spreading out along the edge of the bar, hips pushed forwards so that the butt of the Colt in its holster was well clear of obstruction. The thong at the bottom of the holster was tied tight about Hart's leg. The safety loop by the top was dangling free from the hammer.

There were perhaps a dozen people between Hart and the men who'd come to find him, but he could see their faces clearly enough. They knew who he was now, right enough.

"You lookin' for me?"

Hart's voice wasn't loud, but it was clear and strong. Men at his end of the bar stopped talking abruptly and looked round. The thinner of the bartenders set down a glass carefully and glanced at the sawn-off under the bar. Crazy John Carter turned further round in his chair and Hart could see the black butt of the Colt at his right hip, the white movement of his hand swinging past it, close past it.

"Lookin' for me, John!"

Now more people were conscious of something happening; something about to happen. There was a low murmur of voices, the sound of chairs being hastily pushed back, a clink of glasses. At the other side of the room, the pianist, oblivious, stopped after the final arpeggio of the waltz, cracked his knuckles and went into a piece of fast ragtime.

Crazy John Carter stood up, pushing the right side of his broadcloth coat back with his elbow.

The banjo player gulped in air, set his instrument aside and nudged the pianist's arm. The piano player lost the beat, carried on for several bars, cursed and slammed down the lid. A discordant echo rang out over the room and when it faded it was into silence.

Carter's right hand made a claw that hovered inches above his gun butt. His disfigured eye twitched.

"That's right, Hart. An' now I've found you."

2

WES HART stood clear from the bar, his body dropping naturally into a gunfighter's crouch. His faded blue eyes narrowed on to the figure of Carter, seeing both the snarl on the man's face and the hand close by the gun.

Near the rear of the saloon a chair over-balanced as a man tried to wriggle past into a safer vantage point. One of the girls began to cough, short insistent coughs into the palm of her hand. Somewhere liquid dripped from wood on to wood, the beat of it increasing steadily.

The two who'd been sitting with Carter had moved away from the table, one to either side. Hart could see enough of them to be aware of what they were doing; neither man at the moment making an obvious move towards his weapon, watching closely, waiting.

"It's been a long time, John," said Hart.

Carter stared back at him, one side of his mouth still pulled back in a snarl.

"Didn't know you was holdin' any grudge," said Hart, his voice even, controlled.

Carter's right hand moved slightly, the finger's flexing. Hart's own hand dropped inches nearer to his gun. It was almost touching the pearl handle of the Colt now, his thumb pushed out ready to bring back the hammer.

"What's it to be, John?"

The girl's dry coughs rasped on. Someone started to whisper, stopping abruptly when he realized how loud his voice seemed.

Crazy John Carter's face muscles relaxed, the fingers of his right hand flexed again but this time they moved higher and wide. His mouth played with the beginnings of a grin; his crazy grey eyes flickered a smile.

"Came to talk, Hart. That's it."

Hart moved his tongue along the inside

of his lower lip. "Strange way of goin' about it, John."

Carter let the smile broaden and his head nodded; the smile became a laugh and he lifted both hands midway into the air. "You know they call me Crazy, guess they don't do that for nothin'."

The grey eyes shone and he threw back his head and hollered with laughter, high and edged like a knife blade being drawn along stone.

The man to Carter's right took a step forward. "Come on over," he said. "Let's talk."

Hart hesitated, finally nodded. He turned his head a little, talking to the barman. "Let me have a bottle. An' one more glass."

The taller bartender moved away from where he'd been standing, close by the shotgun, and set the whisky and glass on top of the counter. The silence broke like a rain cloud: men moved away from the sides of the room, talking loudly, insistently, too loudly. The pianist lifted up the lid of his instrument and cracked his knuckles above the keys; the banjo player strummed a chord, then reached for a half-finished drink. A girl in a pale and dirty blue dress stared at the flecks of blood across the inside of her hand.

Hart pulled back the empty chair and waited.

"This here's Moody," said Carter, nodding towards the man with a round, stubbled face. "An' that's Noonan." The man with the broad, strong nose looked back at Hart and nodded briefly.

"Wes Hart." Hart introduced himself and sat down, pulling the top from the bottle and passing it across the table to Moody.

"How d'you know I was here, John?" asked Hart. "Or did you strike lucky?"

Carter laughed quickly. "You weren't hard to find. Not with the sort of reputation you're gettin'."

Hart looked back at the pocked face and made no comment.

"We heard you been holed up here since you rode out of Indian Territory a while back."

"I ain't holed up," said Hart quickly. "I'm just livin'. Ain't hidin' from no one."

Noonan grinned and twisted the whisky glass in his hand. "Way we heard it, there was this US marshal awful keen to clap irons on you and drag you off to Fort Smith."

"Yeah," Moody continued, enjoying it now. "Seems you quit workin' as a deputy an' then sort of ran wild, endin' up shootin' this rancher who took you on. Mighty important man, too."

Hart stared at the two men coldly. "Some folk listen too much. Some folk . . ." and he nodded his head towards Moody, ". . . talk too much."

Moody's face shifted with displeasure and he shifted awkwardly in his chair, but other than that he let the remark ride.

"Whatever happened then," said Carter, "what you doin' now?"

Hart shrugged and reached for the bottle. "Not too much. They had a little trouble here in town an' I cleared it up."

"You ain't no marshal or nothin'?" questioned Noonan.

"No. Ain't nothin'."

"You fixin' to stay that way?" Carter had a smile in his grey eyes and round the edges of his quivering mouth.

"Depends."

Carter sat back and slapped first the edge of the table and then his leg. "Don't it, though," he said with a laugh. "Don't it, just."

Around them most folk had gone back to their own drinking and gambling and were paying the four men little attention. Only one of the barmen cast his eyes towards the centre of the room every now and then, not trusting the peaceful way things had worked out. For one thing, he reckoned he could tell from the three strangers' manner the kind of trouble-makers they were. For another, he'd seen Hart in action. Part of the little trouble Wes Hart had spoken of so lightly.

It had been a couple of weeks back and Hart hadn't long arrived in town. A bunch of miners had ridden down from the north-west and threatened to take the place apart. They'd started in the saloon and then made their drunken way to the whorehouse up the street. Kate Stein had wanted to keep them out altogether but there hadn't been any way she could. At first they'd just been loud and aggressive but finally one of them had started beating up on the girls. The man Kate employed to keep the peace tried to interfere and got shot in the legs for his trouble.

Kate had sent Charlie for the marshal but he was out of town. His deputy was an old timer with a wooden leg and only good for feeding the prisoners and sweeping out the jail.

Finally Kate had gone across to the saloon herself and offered fifty dollars or a month free on the house for any man who'd take the miners on. Wes Hart had done exactly that, offering the bartender a third of the proceeds to stand in the doorway with his shotgun as back-up.

It had been worth it simply to see Hart in action. In less than a couple of minutes he'd put a slug through one man's shoulder, shattered another's elbow, shot one through the back of the calf and pistol whipped another two.

Kate and the bartender had watched open-mouthed in amazement. Hart had looked the girls over, talked with Kate and decided to take his payment in kind. So far it wasn't a decision he regretted.

Now Hart sat easily in his chair and drank some of the whisky and waited for Carter to make his proposition. If he hadn't gone to the trouble of finding him to pick a fight, he had to have had some other good reason.

"Know a place called Tago?" Carter asked eventually.

Hart shook his head.

"Mining town, forty, fifty miles from here," said Moody. "On up into Colorado."

"South of Rattlesnake Buttes," added Noonan.

"Is this important?" asked Hart, looking at Carter. "Or are we just passin' time?"

Carter slapped his thigh once again, laughed again and leaned forward, arms spread across the table. "We come from there. Tago. An' we aim to take you back there."

Hart set down his glass slowly. "Take?"

Carter grinned. "No more'n a way of speakin'."

"Uh-huh. An' why should I be interested in ridin' up to Tago?"

"Money. Good money."

"Doin' what?"

Carter sat back, glanced at Noonan and Moody. "Tago needs a regulator. Hundred and fifty a month an' all found."

"That's a lot of money."

"Top rates."

"How come? The town could hire itself a marshal for maybe half that."

"They tried it," put in Noonan quickly. "Three times."

His expression told Hart clearly enough what had happened. "I still say it's a lot of money."

"Beaumont's a rich man."

"Who's Beaumont? I thought I was bein' hired by a town."

"You are," Carter grinned. "Mason Beaumont is Tago."

Wes Hart glanced round as a couple of men threatened to get into an argument over the play of the cards. When it had blown over he relaxed and accepted another drink from the bottle.

"Maybe this, what's his name, Mason Beaumont, ought to do his own regulating."

Carter pulled his lip back over his uneven teeth as though he was about to let out a howl of amusement, but no sound emerged.

"What's the matter?" asked Moody. "Don't you want to work?"

"I'd need to know more about the job."

"You're awful choosy for a two-bit gunslinger," snapped Moody, letting his annoyance show.

Carter spread his hand towards him. "Steady, now, this ain't no two-bit gun. This here's a hundred-and-fifty-dollar gun."

"An' I'm still sayin' I want to know how come it's worth so much."

Moody pulled his head to one side and pushed his chair back from the table. "Like I want to know what makes you worth so much. You don't seem like nothin' special to me."

"Moody," said Noonan, "you been drinkin' too much."

"You shut your goddamn face!"

The men at the surrounding tables began to glance round apprehensively; one or two of them to edge away. Elsewhere the general clamour persisted.

Carter grinned at Hart. "They're two good boys but when they been at the liquor they get to goadin' one another like a couple of wildcats."

Hart nodded. He noticed that the bottle he'd brought over from the bar was almost dead.

"You goin' to tell me 'bout Tago?" he asked Carter, while the other two continued to utter half-heard threats at each other.

"Nothin' to tell. It's a silver town.

Sprung up Sunday come Monday. Beaumont owns the largest mine an' most of the buildin's in town. Like most places there's been a lot of drinkin' an' whorin', but since he was scoopin' off a profit from most of that he didn't care none. Last few months, though, things been turnin' sour. So much shootin' in town that folk stopped drivin' in for supplies an' went up north for 'em. Then someone started hittin' the mine, stealin' ore, you name it."

Carter turned sharply and glared at his two companions, shutting them up. When he turned back towards Hart he was smiling calmly. At that moment he looked like as sane a man as Hart had ever seen.

"That's where you come in," he said.

Hart shook his head. "No, it ain't."

"What d'you mean?"

"What I say. I ain't interested."

"Why the hell not?"

Hart set both hands to the edge of the table and began to push himself back. "Just ain't."

Something broke at the back of Carter's

grey eyes. "Damn it! That ain't good enough."

Hart stood up—fast. His body was back into a leaning crouch and his hand was clear above the butt of his Colt. All three men stared at him, Moody licking his lips back and across.

The side of Carter's face twitched.

"I'll say it once, John," said Hart. "You boys rode over an' made me a proposition. I turned it down. There ain't no obligation either way. You make sure you understand that. All of you."

Moody's mouth fell open, the tip of his tongue visible. Noonan scratched at the stubble below his chin. Carter continued to stare through cat-like grey eyes. Men behind and to the sides of the table were shifting away, going as fast as they dared without drawing attention to themselves. Pockets of noise were loud in a spreading anticipation.

"I guess it's time you were leavin'," said Hart. He nodded down at the table. "Bottle's mostly gone."

Carter started to move his head from

side to side, still fixing his eyes on Hart and drawing back his upper lip as he did so. "He's not goin' to like this. Beaumont ain't goin' to like this."

Hart looked back at him. "That's his worry. It sure ain't mine."

Behind him someone accidentally backed into a table, sending a glass crashing to the floor. Hart jerked his head sideways, unable to prevent the automatic reaction. As he did so, Carter sprang back from his chair and his right hand swung into an arc that would bring it round to his gun, round and up.

"No!" There was a shout from the side of the room and immediately the crash of a shotgun being fired shook the saloon. Plaster from the ceiling showered over men's heads. Pieces bounced from tables and floor.

Hart's hand was tight about the mother-of-pearl grip of his Colt and the barrel was two-thirds of the way out of its holster. Opposite him, the fingers of Carter's hand were just beginning to close about his pistol butt.

The two men stared at one another through narrowed eyes. Then Carter threw back his head and began his manic laugh, hybrid, out of control. He laughed until tears had started to run down his pock-marked cheeks. When the laughter had finished, Hart was still waiting, his Colt in the same position. Behind his shoulder, the bartender had a fresh charge in the barrels of his shotgun.

"That's twice," said Hart. "Next time you might not be so lucky."

Carter's face twitched angrily. "Next time the luck might not be yours."

Hart nodded and slowly released the hammer, letting the pistol fall back into the holster but keeping his hand near to it. Carter hurled his chair away behind him, sending it crashing into one of the tables. He snarled and began to push his way towards the door, Noonan and Moody following, heads swivelled round to watch Hart.

The three pushed through the bat-wing doors and out into the street. Moments later came the sound of horses riding away. Hart went over to the bar.

"Thanks."

The thin bartender put his head to one side. "Weren't nothin'. You could have taken him anyway."

Hart said nothing, wondering. A man to his left offered to buy him a drink but he refused. The bartender moved away to deal with a customer. The Negro from the whorehouse worked his way to Hart's side.

"What is it, Charlie?"

"Miss Kate, she wants to see you."

"Okay."

Hart turned and followed him out of the saloon and back across the street.

Kate was sitting on a settee in the centre of the room. She was smoking a cigarette, a glass of white wine on the table beside her. Her hair was no longer tied at the back but fell loose about her shoulders, long and dark, lustrous in the orange-yellow light.

"Sit down."

A girl walked slowly downstairs,

combing her fingers through tightly curled red hair. The front of her robe was open and her legs were long and bare. Hart glanced up at her and then away, back at Kate.

"I heard shooting. I was worried."

Hart looked at her questioningly. "It didn't amount to nothing."

"Who were these men? What did they want?"

Hart told her.

She put out her cigarette, half smoked. She picked up the glass and drank some wine. "Why didn't you take the job?"

Hart shrugged.

"You didn't want to leave town?" There was a hint of playfulness in Kate's eyes, in her voice.

"I didn't like the way I was asked. I don't like Crazy John, don't trust him. And I didn't like the sound of Beaumont. I just finished working for a man like him. Too much money and too much greed. I don't want to work for another."

"Who else d'you think is going to employ you, Wes?"

Hart looked away without answering; there wasn't an answer. At least, not one he liked.

She leaned towards him with a swish of her dress and he could smell her scent again. "You didn't have any other reason for not wanting to leave town?" Her voice was soft, almost a mockery of itself.

He shook his head. "No," he said. "None that I could think of."

A smile grew about Kate's dark eyes, then faded. She sat back and reached for her wine. There were lines of condensation down the outside of the glass. For several moments neither of them spoke.

"You want another of my girls?"

Hart stood up. "Not tonight."

"That's good." She looked at him and her face had a hardness which the soft fall of her hair belied. "Your credit here's almost used up."

3

THE odour inside the room was sickly sweet. Warm. Fat, white fingers lifted the bottle from the table and began to remove the stopper. The bottle was small, rounded, violet in colour. While one hand held the bottle, the other took hold of a thick-bottomed glass, half filled with water. Carefully, the neck of the violet bottle was tilted over the glass. The first drop of laudanum fell into the water, spreading. More drops followed, turning the water round, turning it cloudy. One drop more.

Mason Beaumont lifted the glass to his lips. Lips that were loose, almost purple at the edges of the loose, segmented skin. His eyes widened, the pupils small and dark as stones. The head jerked back as the mouth opened, swallowing.

Beaumont's tongue pushed out, licking at the rim of the glass, turning inside it.

At last he sat back heavily in his chair, his arm falling wide. The fingers loosened, parted, and the glass fell to the floor. It landed on its base, wobbled, then was still. It was unbroken.

Beaumont's eyes were closed, his head lolled to one side. Small bubbles of sweat began to form at his temples and along the hair line. A nerve beat rapidly at the right side of his head. He began to breathe heavily, with difficulty, but then within minutes became more controlled. His breathing steadied; the nerve stilled. He could have opened his eyes but had no wish to.

What he could see was more important, more beautiful. The bright light of the sun so bright on the Mississippi that it dazzled the eyes. A great sternwheeler passing up from Memphis. The rich smell of warm earth and the sweetness of pine-wood. The perfume of magnolia in bloom, filling the night air. Melodies of a creole orchestra. Gardenias. Lace.

Someone knocked softly on the door and Beaumont was uncertain where in his reverie it came. The sound rose and faded, rose again, faded, ceased.

Beaumont's head slumped further to one side. After a time his mouth slacked open and a thin sliver of saliva dribbled down his smooth skin and on to the white silk of his shirt.

Jimmy Waterford slapped hard at the mule's rear, moving quickly aside in case the animal should decide to kick back.

"Jesus and Mary! Will you get movin' or what?"

The mule shook its head, long ears flapping; its feet seemed almost embedded in the thick mud of the slope. Each fresh attempt to climb merely made things worse. The bundles roped to the animal's back weighted it down, heavy and cumbersome as they were.

"Jimmy! Are you comin' now?"

Waterford stepped on to a ridge of rock and shielded his eyes from a light that was strong and cold. The sun shone but it shone into puddles of grey rainwater, clogged with reddish-brown mud.

Jimmy's eldest brother, Frank, was standing at the top of the pass, leaning one arm against the side of the grey rock.

"What the hell are you doin'?"

"Tryin' to get this cursed animal to budge up this hill. What d'you think I'm doin"? Prayin'?"

"I thought maybe you was pissin'," laughed Frank. He began to work his way back down, nearly slipping several times.

"It's no use," said Jimmy when his brother was by him. "She isn't goin' to make it."

Frank looked at the load. "We'll have to get this from its back."

Jimmy shook his head, despairingly. "Jesus! It took ages to get it all tied on."

Frank laughed and reached towards one of the knots. "It'll come off easier."

"And what about settin' it all back on again?"

"That'll be okay. Once you've carried it to the top of the pass." He laughed, a good, open laugh, and threaded one end of the rope through and round, reaching another knot.

In ten minutes the brothers had all of the packages stacked on the ground: salt, flour, sugar, dried meat, coffee, cartridges, gunpowder.

"I wonder how Dan's gettin' on?" asked Jimmy.

"He'll be doin' his best, that's all you can say."

Jimmy wiped the sleeve of his shirt across his sweating forehead. "I suppose you're right."

They began to lift the bundles and stagger slowly up the muddy hill, the mule standing fast and shaking its head, watching them with less than understanding.

The Waterfords had come west to Colorado twelve months ago, riding a wagon from New York where their family had lived for five years. Growing up around the Bowery had provided little joy, though none of the lads had starved and they had learnt to be quick and strong in a scrap. Had learned how to dodge bricks and stones, how to parry a knife arm, how to curl into a ball when you were being booted by half a dozen others and how to tease a girl just enough to make her smile and then what to do when she was smiling.

It had been all right while their father had been in work at the brewery, the boys taking jobs when and where they could. But he'd fallen badly and twisted his spine, going down on black ice walking back from his work one December night. After that there'd only been what their mother could make doing cleaning up town and the irregular amounts the brothers brought in.

As winter was fading away to spring, their father went out one night and didn't come back. They found him two days later floating upside down in the river, face partly gnawed away.

Their mother had dragged on until the fall, wearing black, fingering her rosary beads, thin lips for ever mouthing prayer after prayer. One morning she didn't get up at six and set the fire going and when Dan went in to see what was wrong, the fingers of her right hand were set rigidly about the small crucifix that normally hung over her bed.

The boys lived hand to mouth through the winter and started out west almost a year to the day after their father's death.

They'd made a small stake north of Tago and had a little luck, but the work was almost overwhelmingly hard for what they got out. Low as they kept their living expenses, they had to eat; had to use tools; had to contend with the constant harassment of Beaumont's men who didn't like anyone else taking a share of what they thought should be Beaumont's by right. What Beaumont thought should be his.

Right now Dan was in town trying to persuade the bank manager to extend the loan he'd given them six months ago. If he refused it was doubtful how much longer they could hold out without making a big strike.

Jimmy dropped the last package down to the ground and groaned, flexing his arm muscles and stretching his back.

"Take it easy," called Frank, leading

the mule up the hill. "We don't want them things bustin' apart."

"Don't worry, Frank. You're always worryin'. It'll finish you one day, see if it don't."

Frank waved his hand in rebuke and hauled on the rope, dragging the mule clear of another sucking pool of mud.

"It's a wonder we didn't have to carry this dumb beast on our backs as well."

"We may yet," laughed Jimmy. "That we may."

He turned towards his brother and reached out for the end of the rope. As his fingers touched it a rifle shot rang out and a bullet ricocheted off rock a foot above his head.

"Get down!"

Both of them flattened themselves fast, falling headlong into the mud and feeling it splash up around them, splattering over their face and clogging their eyes.

A second shot sniped away and then there came the sound of horses. Frank Waterford pushed himself up on to his hands and knees and wiped his hand across his face, smearing it further.

"The gun! Where's the gun?"

Jimmy rolled over and tugged the heavy Colt Navy from his waistband.

"Give it here!"

Jimmy rolled back and threw the pistol towards Frank, whose hand reached out and grabbed it, fumbling at the butt, almost dropping it altogether.

Through muddied vision he saw three men riding fast towards him and brought up the gun, steadying his aim with the left arm bent under his right. He cocked the gun and fired but apart from the sound of the explosion and the release of smoke, nothing seemed to have happened. The men kept coming.

As they slowed their mounts the two brothers recognized them—they were Beaumont's men.

"Drop it, boy!"

Frank's hand tightened about the grip and he started to bring back the hammer once more. There was a roar and he was toppling sideways, gun thrown aside, clutching at his left arm.

Jimmy sprang up and stopped, seeing the Colt .45 that was levelled at his chest.

"I told you to drop it." Crazy John Carter threw back his head and laughed his raw-edged laugh. "Next time you best listen to what you're told."

Blood seeped through Frank's shirt and between his fingers, falling away towards the ground. More blood ran along the palm of his left hand and trickled into the centre of a grey puddle already swilling with reddish-yellow mud.

"Where you two headin', anyhow?" asked Noonan fiercely.

"That ain't none of your—" Jimmy began, but his brother stopped him.

"We're goin' back to our mine."

"Your mine?" echoed Moody incredulously.

"Sure our mine!" Jimmy slithered to his feet, eyes bright and angry, fists bunched by his sides. He could have been back in the streets of the Bowery, challenging other kids for the right to some pile of ashes.

Carter laughed. "Don't you know this here's Beaumont land?"

"It ain't no one's land," said Frank. "It's just a pile of rock an' mud. It ain't nothin' to nobody."

"Then what you doin' on it?" asked Noonan.

"Takin' supplies to our camp. We told you." Frank Waterford was losing his temper now, too. He knew that they were baiting the pair of them, trying to goad them into something from which it would be impossible to step back, but that didn't make it easy to take. Nor did the pain in his arm help. It was pinching, the nerves drawing in tight in quick spasms as the blood continued to pump through the wound. His hand was sticky with darkening blood; his left leg was splashed by it, his boot freckled through its covering of wet mud.

"You're the Waterfords, ain't you?" asked Moody, thrusting his face towards them, black hat pushed back from his forehead, curly hair hanging forward towards the bridge of his nose.

"Sure we are." Jimmy's bunched fists came up and he glared at the three men with pride. "Sure we're the Waterfords."

Frank's stomach hollowed out. He glanced hastily down at the Colt Navy nestled into the squelched ground. Crazy John Carter followed his glance and let out a manic laugh. His grey eyes shone with excitement; the thin, wide mouth was pulled wider than ever as the laughter grew and grew.

Noonan and Moody freed their gun hands from the reins, sensing that Carter was about to explode over the edge.

Frank Waterford could see it, too, but he wasn't certain how to avert it. As the laugh was still ringing between the slabs of rock, Frank pointed across to his brother. "Come on, Jmmy, let's get these things loaded up and be on our way."

He turned away from the three men and took a couple of unsteady steps in the direction of the mule.

Jimmy hesitated, uncertain.

"You Irish bastard!" roared Carter. "Don't you turn your back on me!"

"Frank! Look out!"

As his brother's warning spun him round, Frank saw the pistol coming up from Carter's side and his mouth opened to shout words that never came. The gun fired twice, one shot merging into the other. Frank was hurled backwards, one of his feet up in the air, arm flailing wildly, two bullet holes torn through the left side of his chest. His body slapped down into the mud and water splashed up around him. He rolled to one side but fell back again, unable to move.

Jimmy Waterford stared at his brother, lips set tight together, eyes wide with shock and fear.

"That'll teach you!" Carter crowed. "That'll teach you to turn your back on Crazy John Carter!"

Jimmy turned his head and looked up at Carter. His eyes brimmed with sorrow and hate. He saw the Colt Navy on the ground and leaped towards it, diving into the mud and through it, right hand reaching out desperately.

Carter smiled and swung his horse around so that his right side was towards the youngster. He watched as Waterford's fingers closed about the heavy butt of the gun and tightened, watched as Jimmy's arm swivelled and lifted, watched the expression in the white face.

He aimed quickly and squeezed the trigger.

Jimmy felt as if something had kicked him in the ribs, something invisible, hard in the middle of his ribs. His back slammed into the rock at the side of the hill and almost immediately he choked up a gout of fresh, bright blood. He stared at it in disbelief, bright and fresh on the ground between his legs. He coughed harshly. Through watering eyes he looked for the pistol that should have been in his hand but was no longer there. He tried to look at the man who'd shot him but all he could see was a blurred shape which shifted back and forth across his vision.

Jimmy's head dipped down and

suddenly he was taking in thick, muddy water through his mouth and nose. Choking in it. He tried to push himself up but there didn't seem to be any strength in his arms. His head came six inches off the ground and almost immediately sank down again.

He could hear laughter and voices and he strained to listen, to listen to what they were saying because he was convinced it must be important. Words moved across his mind without catching, horses moved close to him and he tried to pull his arms above his head to protect it, thinking they were going to ride over him, trample him deeper into the mud.

The voices faded and the hoofbeats seemed to be more and more distant. The pain in his chest was like a saw now, the kind he and Dan had used to cut up firewood back on one of the lots in New York. Trundling it round the streets in an old pram, calling out, selling it for what they could get. He could see the saw, see the blade, the rusting teeth clearly; feel it driving jaggedly between his ribs. He opened his mouth to scream and blood flooded the puddle in which he was laying.

Voices: the voices came back. Quarrelling, loud, saying things he didn't want to hear. Blaming. Blame. Blame. And now softer, a woman's voice saying a prayer. Hail Mary, full of grace, the Lord is with thee . . .

Jimmy trembled through his whole body. It couldn't be his mother's voice. No. Not there. His mother couldn't be there. His mother was . . .

The mule stood where it was for some time, waiting for either of the two men to move from where they were laying on the muddy ground. When they didn't, it slowly wandered off, idly searching for food.

Lacy sat in the rocker on the porch of the Beaumont house, reading the St. Louis paper. It was more than a week old but that didn't matter. News was news and news was interesting. He sat upright in the chair, not rocking it but maintaining balance. The newspaper was folded lengthways, once and then again. Lacy read it through wire-framed spectacles, their round frames seeming quite in place on his mild, pale face.

It was almost as if, had the spectacles not been there, his face would have been featureless.

He wore a neatly tailored grey suit with a thin cream stripe running through the material; a cream coloured vest with silver buttons and a silver watch chain looped from the vest pockets. A couple of inches of clean, white shirt cuff showed past the ends of his coat sleeves and the collar of the shirt was buttoned tight.

Lacy turned the paper and refolded it, finding the second column of news about mining stocks. As he refolded the newspaper, he uncrossed his knees and then recrossed them the other way about. The crease in his pants leg was level and the shine of his black shoes was recent and bright.

He looked over the top of the paper when he heard the riders approaching, waiting until he'd identified them before returning to his reading.

He continued to read as they brought their lathered mounts to a halt and jumped down from the saddles, tying the horses to the hitching rail in front of the porch.

"Hey, Lacy!"

Lacy waited until he had finished the paragraph he was reading before lowering the newspaper and acknowledging the men.

"Tell you, Lacy, we just killed ourselves a couple of trash miners. Up there on the mountain."

Crazy John Carter squinted up at Lacy and giggled, the top of his body twitching nervously. He put the outside of his hand to his mouth and bit at it, head shaking.

Lacy folded the paper and set it carefully on the floor beneath the legs of the rocker.

"Where is he?" he asked mildly.

"Didn't you hear what I said?" demanded Carter. "We just—"

"Where is he? In town at the hotel?"

"He didn't come," said Noonan flatly.

Lacy peered at him through his spectacles. "You mean he didn't ride in with you? He had business to attend to and he'll be followin' on."

Noonan shook his head. "No. I mean he ain't comin'."

Lacy put his hands together in front of his face, palms apart, fingers barely touching. "Not at all."

"That's what I said."

Lacy began to propel the rocker with his feet, moving it slowly, evenly. "Mr. Beaumont isn't going to like this. He isn't going to like this at all."

Carter snarled and went close to the end of the porch; the cast in his left eye was more noticeable than ever. Below it the side of his face was twitching as he bit down on the inside of his thin-lipped mouth.

"To hell with that! What does it matter? Why don't you listen to what I'm telling you? We run into two of them bastard Irish and gunned 'em down."

"Without reason?" Lacy's question was mild.

"They was trespassin'," put in Noonan.

"An' one of 'em went for a gun," added Carter excitedly. "He was goin' to use it on me." His eyes widened in mock surprise. "What else could I do?"

Lacy stopped the movement of the chair with the flat of his shoe. "You could have done what you were sent to do. You could have brought back the regulator."

Carter's right arm shot into the air, his fist grabbing and punching as if he was scarcely able to contain his anger. "To hell with it, Lacy! To hell with you forever tellin' me what to do! I ain't goin' to take it. I ain't!"

Moody and Noonan recognized the moment and began to back away. Carter's right hand stopped punching air and dived down, spreading as it came. His fingers were inches above the butt of his Colt when Lacy's right hand emerged from inside his coat. There was a Smith and Wesson .38 steady in his grip.

Nothing else about him had changed—his expression behind the wire-framed spectacles was as bland as before—only the gun. Even the voice was as mild.

"If you give me opportunity enough, Carter, I'm going to have to kill you. But in the meantime I think the three of you should find some way of scraping the mud off your boots and step inside. I'm sure Mr. Beaumont would like to speak with you."

4

MASON BEAUMONT leaned back in the white leather chair, annoyed at having been disturbed. His pinkish face was drawn in about the mouth; the pupils of his eyes were small and rounded, dark. The thin cigar in his left hand sent a wraith of smoke up towards the ceiling. Tiny flecks of ash were specked down the front of his white suit.

The room was painted white, framed paintings and daguerreotypes hung from the walls, along with sabres and sashes and other military paraphernalia. Immediately behind Beaumont's head was a portrait, half life size, of his father in the full dress uniform of a major of the Army of the Confederacy. The black-bearded face was suitably stern beneath a grey hat with a blue-grey plume which rose from the left side of the crown to curl over the rear of the brim. The collar and buttons of the coat were yellow, as was the ornate piping on the sleeves. A yellow sash hung from the side of the belt, down the light blue trousers and almost touching the tops of the polished knee boots. The sabre, hanging low and angled from the leather belt, was the same one that now hung from two wooden pegs in the wall.

The subject of the painting lay beneath a marble monument in Nashville, Tennessee.

His son had not fought in the war between the states. Mason Beaumont had been commissioned but he had not fought.

He looked up at Lacy and nodded. "You'd better get them in, if you must."

Lacy went to the door and held it open as Carter and the other two walked through. Carter seemed more controlled now, only the expression in his eyes suggesting otherwise. The three of them approached Beaumont uneasily, Noonan with his hat hanging down behind his head as usual, Moody with his in his left hand.

"What went wrong, Carter?" Beaumont's voice was thin and slightly squeaky, like a door that was in need of oil.

"They were tres—"

The altered look in Beaumont's face stopped him, told him he was wrong. He licked his upper lip and started again.

"We found him okay. Hart. Told him everything just like you said. He didn't want to do it, Mr. Beaumont. Didn't want to work for you."

A length of ash fell away from the end of Beaumont's untouched cigar.

"He didn't want to work for me? You explained everything to him and he didn't want to work for me?"

Crazy John Carter nodded. "That's right, Mr. Beaumont. Wasn't anythin' we could do, not without . . ." He left the rest of it unsaid.

Pink fingers reached out for the cigar and crushed it, flakes of dark tobacco crumbling about the rounded finger ends, the polished nails.

"That man," he said slowly, "that shootist needs to learn some manners." He flicked the ash from his hand. "You're going back."

Noonan and Moody looked at one another quickly. Carter nodded, then allowed a smile to appear on his face as he thought of the consequences.

Beaumont looked past him. "Lacy, I think you'd better go with them."

Lacy put his hand to his face and removed his spectacles, folding them and slotting them down into the breast pocket of his coat. "With respect, Mr. Beaumont, this might not be the best of times for me to be away."

"How d'you mean?"

"The two Waterford brothers that Carter, er, killed. There is a third brother. From what I hear he's headstrong, determined . . ."

Beaumont gestured with his hand. "I understand." His gaze returned to Carter.

"Go back to this man. Give him one more chance to accept my terms."

Carter's grey eyes were alive: "What if he won't?"

Beaumont let his head fall back against the soft leather of his chair; his voice was soft as a whisper. "Kill him," he said. "Kill him."

Wes Hart let the coins fall from one hand to the other, the soft metallic chink of money. It wouldn't be too long before the cash he'd taken from the Jackson place in Indian Territory was all used up. Before that happened he'd have to get himself another job and that might not be too easy. Maybe he'd been a fool to turn down the one at Tago.

Hart shook his head. There was something about Crazy John Carter that made him want to keep as much distance between Carter and himself as possible. And any man who'd employ someone like Carter, as Beaumont apparently had, wasn't a person whose judgement Hart trusted a great deal.

He slipped the coins back into the cotton bag and pulled the draw strings tight. It didn't make sense thinking about it now—Beaumont would have found himself another man.

Hart buckled on his gunbelt, giving the Colt the usual heft and spin before slipping the safety loop over the hammer, tied the thong about his leg, and went out of the room.

He nodded to the few people sitting around the foyer of the hotel and stepped on to the boardwalk. The sunlight was strong, causing him to pull the brim of his flat-crowned black hat down over his eyes. A hay wagon trundled past, drawn by a pair of shaggy brown mules, a boy of no more than ten sitting up behind them and encouraging them along with whistles and shouts. A tall woman carrying a parasol paused outside the draper's shop and looked into the window. Reflected there, she saw Hart looking at her and swung round quickly, her face showing displeasure. Hart turned away.

He thought he'd fetch his horse from the livery stable and take a ride up into the wooded hill country north of the town. Last time he'd been there he'd spotted a black bear up above the line of the pines, its brown face peering back down at him, small dark eyes staring past the straight nose. The black of its coat veered towards cinnamon in places. Hart and the bear had looked at one another for quite some time, each summing the other up and finally deciding it best to keep out of the way. There had been something honest and direct about it—not like the woman over by the draper's store.

"Wes."

He swung his head at the voice. Kate Stein had come out of the store and was now heading in the same direction as himself, though across the street.

She waved a gloved hand at him, unaware of the look of disdain, hatred almost, being given her by the woman with the parasol. Or perhaps she wasn't unaware; perhaps she just didn't care.

Hart liked her for that. It was one of the things he liked her for.

He considered waiting for Kate to catch up with him and walking along with her, but instead he just acknowledged the wave with a gesture of his right hand to the brim of his hat and carried on his way.

He saddled up the animal quickly, finally letting the stirrups fall down from the seat of the Denver saddle and tightening the cinch.

In one of the stalls down to Hart's right, a horse snickered loudly and banged its hoofs against the wooden slats. A rake, or something similar, fell to the ground. Hart slipped the toe of his left boot into the stirrup, left hand tight on the curve of the saddle pommel.

"Hart."

The voice came from behind and he spun fast, his body turning and his hand arching downwards towards his holster. The big Colt came up smoothly and cleanly, thumb bringing back the hammer, arm angling the gun upwards towards the upper storey.

"Hart."

He pulled his boot clear of the stirrup and dropped into a crouch. A different voice this time and further round the gallery, behind ropes and tackle and bales of hay.

Hart moved, cat-footed, towards the nearest empty stall, listening for either man to move.

"Hart."

A third voice and this one he recognized: they had come back.

"John. Crazy John Carter."

"You called it, Hart."

He was by the double doorway, tall doors, rounded at the top, big enough for a loaded hay wagon to drive through with ease. One of the doors was fastened to, and Carter's voice seemed to be coming from somewhere behind that.

"What d'you want, John?"

Hart was looking around the inside of the stables. There was a ladder five yards to his left, another fifteen yards to his right, close to the far wall. Both led up to the half-floor above. A side door, beyond the second ladder, was shut and could be locked.

"Same as before, Hart." Carter's voice sounded strained, uneasy, as if it was about to break. Hart thought that if it did it would be into that laugh of his and that after that happened the shooting would follow fast. He didn't fancy having to move forward and show his back to two men up above.

"Call your men out, Carter, then we can talk."

The laugh started, choking off after a few seconds. "We already did that. We talked already. All you got to say is yes or no."

A board creaked directly over Hart's head and he ducked, staring up. The dark shape of a man pulled back behind a block of something solid. Light came thinly through the space between the planks of wood.

"We ain't waitin' all day, Hart."

Someone was approaching the stables,

whistling and leading some kind of wagon. Hart could distinguish the rattle and squeak of the rig. As he listened, the whistling stopped abruptly and the wagon with it. Hart slipped out of the stall and began to edge along towards the right-hand ladder and the side door. His boots pushed through the straw. Again, a horse snickered and kicked.

There was the sound of something heavy falling outside.

"Yes or no, Hart, that's all you got!"

Hart held his breath and continued towards the ladder; it was less than a dozen feet away now.

"John, he's movin'!"

Hart turned from the waist and brought up his Colt. He saw the movement along at the other end of the gallery and fired once, fast.

His shot splintered the edge of a post and whined away towards the roof. Two guns answered him and he ducked back fast, close by a big chestnut mare, who tossed her mane and stared at him balefully.

Carter's voice called out over the fading sound of gunfire. "That your answer, Hart?"

"That's it."

He ran past the ladder towards the door. A shell tore through the top corner of it as his left hand gripped the handle. Another slammed into the floor close by his feet. The handle refused to turn; the door was locked. Through the boards he could see bales of hay piled close against it. Two more shots sounded from behind.

Hart dived full length into the loose beginnings of a pile of straw. Breath was pushed out of his body. His elbow jarred badly. Another shot sought him out. He rolled to the left, over and over, into the straw. A figure began to descend the ladder at the other end of the stable. Hart stopped rolling and lay flat, bringing up the Colt in front of his face. He aimed fast and squeezed down on the trigger.

The slug drove through Noonan's upper arm, making him yell out and let go of the rifle in his hand. The butt of the Winchester hit the ground with a thud and Hart fired a second time. Noonan rocked back against the ladder, a bullet wound clean through his side, below the rib cage. He waved his left arm wildly, then opened his mouth in a helpless scream. He pitched forwards on to the ground, the hard floor stopping his mouth fast.

Hart sprang to his feet and jumped towards a couple of crates close by the front wall of the stable. A shot from another rifle followed him, ricocheting away from the corner of the top crate.

"You ain't gettin' out of here," Carter called. "Not now. Not alive, you ain't."

Hart ignored him, trying to work out where Moody was on the gallery. He thought he could separate out the man's shadow from the other dark shapes and wasted a shell proving himself wrong. He cursed under his breath, worked the ejector rod on the Colt and fingered fresh shells from the loops on his gunbelt and into the chambers.

"Too bad you didn't see it my way, Hart." Carter's voice was tinged with laughter. "Too bad you chose the wrong damned way.

There was no mistaking Crazy John Carter's excitement, the joy at what he was saying. His laugh rose, jagged and high, up towards the roof of the stable.

"Hart, you picked yourself the route to hell!"

Hart scowled and racked his brain trying to figure out what was making Carter so infernally happy with himself. It only took a couple of moments before he found out. There was a loud crash of glass in the middle of the floor and almost immediately the sound of gunfire. Flame burst up from the smashed kerosene lantern Carter had hurled into the stable and something went splashing close to it.

Hart knew at once what it was: Carter was throwing more kerosene from a can. Throwing it over the wood, the dry straw, alongside the horses' stalls.

"Carter, you crazy bastard!"

Hart edged his gun round the crate and fired twice but Carter was back beyond range. He started to move round, eager to rush the door. A rifle shot from on high sent him ducking back down.

"Carter!"

The only answer was the laugh, weird through the crackle and leap of flame.

"Carter, you madman, what the hell you done?" The voice was Moody's, aware now that he was trapped, too, just as Hart was. Even worse, cut off on the half-floor above.

"Carter, get me out of here!"

Moody had lost caution in his new-found fear. Hart angled up his Colt and squeezed back on the trigger. The gun jumped against the steadiness of his hand and Moody was sent slamming back against the wall, a slug through his shoulder. Blood spurted through the ragged hole then trickled unsteadily. Moody bit down on his lower lip and tried to bring up the Winchester. Hart saw the movement and fired again. This time he hit Moody in the hip, the slug deflecting off the chipped bone, upwards through his chest and lodging between two ribs. Moody shook and swayed and staggered towards the edge. The rifle fell from his grasp and bounced on the floor below.

The flames were at head height now and spreading. Animals were kicking against their stalls and whinnying loudly in panic. Hart coughed on the smoke and put his left arm across his face against the rising heat.

Moody toppled on the edge of the gallery, then fell forward, one arm coming out in a vain effort to break the fall. The arm broke instead. Hart heard it crack seconds before the heavy thump of the man's body. Moody landed first on arm, shoulder and head, rolling a little to one side before being still. His legs were spread-eagled behind him; blood ran out from beneath his body towards the fire.

"Too bad, Hart!" shrieked Carter. "Too damned bad!"

Hart ran low towards his horse, which had hurried to the side of the stable and was shying away in terror, joining its noise to that of the other animals. Hart had one hand on the mare's nose to quieten her when he heard what might be a fire bell ringing further back along the street.

He pulled himself up into the saddle and swung the animal's head round towards the centre of the fire.

"Come on, Clay! Come on!"

The big grey reared up and fought; Hart held the reins fast and dug his knees into her sides, kicking into her with his heels. Wisps of blazing straw sailed over their heads. The sound of men's voices was louder now and the ringing of the bell was clear and insistent.

The front wall of the stable had caught fast and was like a wall of flame around the high door. As the grey bucked and wheeled beneath Hart's body, a couple of shots rang out from the far side of the fire's centre.

"Clay! Come on! Through! Through!"

He slapped at her flank with his open hand and kicked hard. Head to one side the mare charged at the flames, heading for the rear edge of the fire where there was still a small gap between flames and the stall along the back wall. Hart flung up an arm to protect his face and swivelled his body away from the searing heat.

The horse jumped through and immediately slewed right, heading for the doorway. Beyond the arc of fire Hart could see a chain of men forming with buckets and at the far side of the street more men were turning the water wagon.

Hart stared around for sign of Carter, but he couldn't pick him out. People were milling around, shouting orders and counter orders; children raced between the line of men passing buckets and shrieked and waved their arms. A group of women stood together down the street from the water wagon, pointing and talking excitedly. From inside the stable came the high, terrified sound of the horses.

Hart rode the grey a little way down the street, folk looking at him as he went, speculating on what had gone on inside. He slipped from the saddle and tried to calm the mare down, stroking her nose and talking to her quietly at the same time as looking up and down the street. Carter could have ridden away when the first of the firemen appeared, but Hart didn't think that likely.

He looped the reins about the hitching post and stepped on to the boardwalk.

"Hart!"

He heard the hissed name and flung himself to the ground, twisting as he went. A pistol roared from the store window behind him, shattering the plate glass to smithereens. Pain lanced along Hart's back and he winced as he struck the boards heavily with his left arm. Rolling fast, right hand clawing for his Colt, he saw Carter in the centre of the window, standing in the middle of sacks of flour, jars of peaches and plums, cans of beans and beef. His mouth was twisted in a macabre laugh, grey eyes staring at Hart, hate and anger strong within them.

The hammer of Hart's Colt came back as Carter fired his second shot. The report of Hart's gun merged with it. A slug tore through the planking inches away from Hart's left arm.

Crazy John Carter staggered back against a stack of crates with his hand clutching at his side. Hart's shot had gone home close to the edge of his ribs, smashing one and deflecting upwards to exit near his armpit. He struggled to bring up his gun arm as Hart got to his feet.

Men were running down towards them, away from the fire.

Carter stumbled forward, kicking against lines of jars and sending them crashing on top of one another. He lurched wildly and a sack of flour plummeted down. The pock-marked face was contorted with pain.

Hart cocked the Colt and took a pace nearer.

"Beaumont sent you back, huh?"

Crazy John's head nodded strangely, small dipping movements, the grey eyes opening and closing. The thin mouth widened into the laugh Hart knew so well and the cast in the left eye twitched rapidly.

"Sent me back to kill you." Carter

seemed to think it was funny. He rocked back and forth on his feet, blood falling away from his side and staining the spilled white of the flour. The laugh rose and rose, became sharper and sharper. Folk standing in an arc around the scene stared at him in amazement.

"... kill you!"

Crazy John Carter made a final effort to bring up his gun as he screamed defiance. Hart shot him twice, the two bullets so close together they formed a single wound. Carter's body was lifted off its feet and flung back against the crates. His arms spread wide and his head drooped. Blood came freely from the great gash in his chest. He wobbled forwards again, turned, buckled, fell.

Hart released the hammer on the Colt and slipped it back down into his holster. Crazy John Carter was sprawled across the window, one leg sticking out on to the boardwalk. His face lay in a pool of syrup that had run from several smashed peach jars. Flour dusted his clothes. The clear syrup and the milled flour were rapidly becoming dark, red.

Hart turned away, expressionless. The pain from the wound in his back was biting into him, biting deep. He gritted his teeth and narrowed his eyes, straightening himself before walking through the crowd.

As he walked away a loud crash made him turn his head: the front and one side wall of the livery stable had come to the ground. Presumably the bodies of Noonan and Moody were still inside. At least that took care of their burial. Hart wondered if anybody would do the same for Carter.

Some men he'd had to kill, that was a responsibility he'd taken upon himself. He'd had to kill and had regretted it. But not Crazy John—you didn't waste time preaching words over mad dogs set to rest too late.

Hart saw Kate Stein in the doorway of her place, one hand resting on her hip. She opened her mouth to say something, but thought better of it. Instead she walked across the street towards him, taking his arm and leading him in the direction of her door, leading him gently but firmly. Hart didn't feel he was about to argue.

5

THE bullet had ploughed a line nearly an inch deep along the left side of Hart's back, starting a few inches above the buttock and continuing until the shoulder. It had carved out a straight channel, grazing the blade bone and causing Hart to lose quite a lot of blood.

The doctor had cleaned the wound thoroughly and strapped it up tight, telling Hart he had to spend a couple of days at least in bed.

After one of those days, Hart was restless and bored. Kate kept telling him he had to stay put and do what the doctor had said, but still he didn't like it. It was one thing to be in bed in a whorehouse of your own free will, quite another to be there as a patient and not even allowed to take advantage of the amenities.

Evie was in the room now, sitting in a

chair next to the bed working on her sampler. The words, *Home is Where the H . . .* stood out in scarlet thread, while Evie worked to finish the last words in time to send it to her mother for her birthday.

Earlier, she'd chattered away to Hart about how she'd left home in Kansas and hoped to make a career for herself on the stage. How she'd got a job singing in a chorus line of six other girls on a tour of the middle west. The six had become four. In Omaha the manager had absconded with what little takings existed and left the troupe stranded. They'd tried to carry on by themselves, but inside a month the line consisted of Evie. Solo can-can wasn't a big draw—not big enough to pay a girl's expenses. She'd been sitting on her upended trunk outside a stage station when she'd met Kate. Since then she hadn't looked back, she hadn't gone hungry and she'd sent her mother little presents from time to time accompanied by notes telling her how well she was doing and that now she was playing juvenile leads in musical comedy.

Now she sat there with her own thoughts, working the sampler painstakingly, small dark eyes flicking along the path of the needle.

Hart eased his back into the deep pillows and tried not to think of anything other than what he was going to do when he got out of there and was able to climb into the saddle again. He wasn't always successful; other thoughts interceded. Images confused him—what had been his home until as a young kid he up and quit—what might have been his home except that the woman he'd planned to share it with . . .

"Wes. How're you feeling?"

Kate stepped inside, balancing a tray on the flat of her hand. "I brought you some soup. You've got to keep up your strength you know."

Hart nodded and mumbled something and Kate glanced quickly at Evie, her larger darker eyes holding the girl's for a few seconds before dismissing her. Evie looked down at her sampler, then stood up.

"'Bye, Wes. I'll be sure to come in and see you again."

She smiled briefly and left the room, shutting the door quietly behind her. Kate sat down next to the head of the bed and set the tray on Hart's lap. The soup was thick and smelled of beef, steam rising from it; several pieces of bread were laid alongside.

"How are you feeling?"

"Feelin' I've been here too long,"

"It's hardly any time at all."

He looked at her. "There's things to do."

Kate opened her mouth, a sight of her pale tongue between white, even teeth. She held on to the words, knowing it would be useless to say them, worse than useless. Not even sure if they were things she wanted to say because they were meant or because she somehow reckoned she ought to say them.

"How's your soup?" she asked after a while.

Hart nodded, mouth full, looking at her again. Her dark hair was pulled back tight. She was wearing a black dress that fitted her body close. Round, silver earrings hung alongside her fine-boned face. A thin silver bracelet circled her left wrist; a small cameo ring on the second finger of the left hand. Around her neck, between the rise of her breasts, hung a silver heart-shaped locket.

Hart banged the spoon against the side of the bowl, dropped it back down. "Tomorrow. I'm leavin' tomorrow. First light."

"You're not . . ." She caught herself, stopped.

"Get Charlie to see to my horse. Pick me up some supplies. Okay?"

Kate nodded, taking the tray from his lap.

"I think I might be movin' on myself soon."

Hart looked surprised. "How come?"

She set her head a little to one side. "I get restless. Besides, some of the decent folk around town aren't very happy with this place any longer." She pronounced decent as if it were a very dirty word.

"Why the hell not? It's clean, well run, successful."

Kate stood up. "Exactly."

She bent down to lift the tray and her face came close to his. Just for a moment. Then she was moving towards the door.

At the doorway she turned her head. "If you're going tomorrow you'd best get all the rest you can." She paused, looking at him. "If you're leaving that early I probably won't see you. Good luck, Wes."

He thought she added something else that might have been, "Take care", but by then the door was closing and the words were muffled. Hart leaned back and closed his eyes.

The river gorge struck through the mountains, a flash of blue reflecting here and there from the sinuous line of water. Down on either side of the river patches of bright grass alternated with sandy mud. The cliffs to the east were bare of vegetation, crumbled and broken surfaces of grey and brown and the occasional red. At the other side of the valley the slope was more gradual; shades of green merged into hazy blue at the top. Pines stood alone or in small clumps; there were patches of dark scrub lower down and above midway, where the ground levelled out for a spell, the yellow tops of aspens moved in the wind.

Hart straightened the brim of his hat and spoke softly to the grey, which went into a walk, picking her path with care. The wind was strong, keen at that height. He had unrolled his Indian wearing blanket from behind his saddle and slipped it over his right shoulder so that it hung diagonally across his body and was knotted below his left hip. The blanket was woven from hand-spun dark blue, red and white wool yarns, striped with a row of star shaped patterns along the centre and at the edges.

Hart had been carrying the blanket for some ten years, ever since it had been presented to him by a Navajo chief at the time he'd been working as an Indian scout for the army.

The double-edged knife which hung from his saddle pommel was in an Apache sheath which had been given to him a couple of years earlier, before he'd moved north.

He had another weapon which went further back, which came from another time he recalled with mixed feelings. In the right side saddlebag was a Starr double-action .44 pistol he'd taken from a Union soldier during the Civil War. The time he'd been riding under the colours of General Henry Hopkins Sibley on the General's rampaging expedition through Albuquerque and Santa Fé. That had been before their luck had changed; before the superior strength of Union arms and men had beaten them back, broken them—broken some of them.

The grey pulled up and tossed its head. A mule deer, its coat changing from blue-grey to reddish-brown, stood on a ledge thirty yards off, staring at man and rider. Its large, leaf-shaped ears were raised in front of high arching antlers, eyes oval and dark and bright.

Hart clicked his tongue against the roof of his mouth to set the horse in motion again and at the sound the deer turned fast and ran along the uneven rock, its black-tipped tail showing clearly against the white rump.

Within seconds it had disappeared from sight. Hart smiled to himself and started to whistle a fragment of a tune he'd heard once down on the Mexican border. When they rounded the next bend he stopped abruptly. There it was laid out below: Tago.

The town was at the end of the gorge, before the mountains closed in and shut off everything but the river. The buildings were mostly clustered in a rough circle on the western bank, though a few straggling places had appeared on the other side. From that distance it was impossible to pick out features, shapes, enough to see that it was growing into a town of fair size.

Above Tago the trees had been cleared

for a width of maybe five hundred yards and set into the middle of that bare patch were mine workings. Smoke spiralled up towards the cold blue of the sky in a lazy movement that seemed almost frozen in time. As Hart got nearer he could pick out other, smaller workings, wooden props around openings in the rock, wooden shacks, wagons. More smoke came from along the eastern ledge.

Silver, thought Hart. Silver.

His face set in a grimace, his eyes narrowing and the line of his mouth fine and tight. He'd seen mining towns before, worked them. Something about the craze for instant riches burned its way into everyone's blood, even the ones that weren't themselves up there digging, blasting, sifting.

The buildings took on shape, colour. Round the outskirts a succession of grey tents flapped in the wind, strong enough even at the foot of the valley. Single-storey shacks gave way to taller, more substantial buildings. The mud-caked, dry street led into a square: the Silver Star

Saloon, long and painted silver and blue across its front, a balcony above; the Tago Mining Company Assay Office, Mason Beaumont, Proprietor, in smaller letters beneath its main sign; Bank of Tago, Mason Beaumont, Prop.; Beaumont Dry Goods and Suttlers . . .

Hart stopped looking—he'd seen enough.

He rode over towards the saloon and slipped to the ground, looping the reins over the hitching rail between six or seven other horses already there. On the boardwalk he slowly turned full circle. Faces stared at him from other points of the square. From the window of the store, from the doorway of the bank, from the upstairs of the assayers. A loose board above made him glance up at the balcony. A woman with bright red hair and wearing a green robe with feathers stitched to the hem, looked back down at him without interest.

Hart flicked the safety thong clear of the hammer of his Colt and pushed through the bat-wing doors and into the saloon. Maybe a dozen people inside stopped what they were doing and turned to face him. Hart hesitated a moment, letting them see what they wanted to see, then moved over to the bar. Grease and dust were thick on the counter. The man who came slowly to serve him was unshaven and bleary-eyed; the apron tied above his waist was ringed with dark stains. He wiped the back of one hand over his mouth before speaking.

"What you drinkin'?"

"Beer."

"Okay." The barkeep poured a glass of yellowy liquid with an inch head of foam and slopped it down on the bar.

Hart stared at him a moment, then took a coin from his pocket and dropped it deliberately down into the wet. He lifted the glass and drank: it was as bad as it looked.

"Wanna buy yourself a piece of land?" The man who'd come up alongside Hart was short and thin, strands of wispy hair arching over his balding head. His thick plaid shirt was torn at one arm; his face disfigured by a virulent purple swelling on his right cheek.

"Up on the mountain. Claim all staked out." He fumbled in his pocket and tried to pull clear a piece of paper. "'S all legal. Right . . . right here." He finally flourished the paper, tatty at the edges, under Hart's nose. "Let you have it for hundred dollars."

The small watering eyes looked at Hart with some vestige of hope. "Seventy-five, that's as low as I'll go. Sev . . . fifty dollars, mister. You can't do better'n that. Fifty dollars for . . ."

Hart fished in his pocket and fingered out a coin, reaching forward and dropping it down into the man's shirt pocket. "Here," he said. "You keep your mine."

The man bristled back. "Hey, mister. I ain't beggin', I'm sellin'. I ain't got no need to beg. Not me. No way I need to . . ."

Hart turned away and moved a few chairs out of the way getting to an unoccupied table. He sat down and leaned the chair back on to its rear legs, stretching out. As soon as he'd finished his beer he'd go off and get something to eat. Time enough to find Beaumont when he'd looked around. It didn't seem as if Mason Beaumont was going to be too hard to find anyway—not the way he was leaving his name all over town.

He watched as the man who'd been trying to sell him what was likely a worthless piece of paper leaned across the bar and used the coin Hart had given him to buy a drink.

That was always the way it was. Especially in places like this.

The doors swung open and a thickset man walked in briskly, followed by another, tall and thin and wearing a neat grey suit. The first man stopped short of the bar and jabbed a finger in the direction of the bartender. "Bottle of whisky and glasses. Bring 'em over."

His voice was gravelly, deep. His mouth red above a full beard. Hart put him at around forty-five. Without waiting for the bartender to start obeying his order but assuming that he would, the man walked towards the back of the room. He went close by Hart without giving him a second glance.

His companion, however, found Hart more interesting. Interesting enough to take a pair of spectacles from his pocket and set them on his nose, staring through them for some little time until his friend called him over.

Hart stared back, unconcerned, wondering if the slight bulge underneath the left side of the man's coat was a gun and if so whether he ever got to use it.

"Lacy, you comin'?"

His pale face having given nothing away, the thin man nodded briefly and walked slowly past Hart, glancing down at him as he passed. Not exactly at him—at the pearl-handled Colt .45 in his holster.

Hart waited a while, then screwed his chair round so that he could see the pair at the table without setting his back towards the door. The bearded man was doing most of the talking—shouting—and the other one sat there calmly, listening, nodding, from time to time gesturing with his right hand.

Hart wondered if the bearded one was Mason Beaumont, but somehow he wasn't certain. It was almost as if this man was being too loud, too pushy. If you owned as much as Beaumont did then you didn't have to shout about it. Not in a saloon like this, you didn't.

"Jesus!" The bearded man pushed back his chair and hurled the contents of his glass across the floor. "What in hell's name d'you call this mule's piss? Whisky?"

Several heads turned towards him, but nobody seemed too surprised. Hart guessed they were used to such outbursts.

"You!" A hand pointed at the bartender. "You! I'm talkin' to you. You hear me?"

"I hear you well enough, Mr. Henry." The barman's voice was weary, disinterested in the whole business.

"Then do somethin' about it. Fetch us a bottle of somethin' decent, not this pisswater!" He got hold of the bottle and threw it with a sideways swing of the arm, sailing it over the heads of two men playing cards and smashing it against the side wall.

The bartender sighed and brought a fresh bottle, putting it on the table with exaggerated care.

The man with spectacles sat through this performance unperturbed, occasionally pressing the tips of his fingers together for seconds at a time. When Hart looked away he noticed that somebody else had slipped into the saloon during the episode and was standing at the end of the bar nearest to the doors.

He was young, likely not more than twenty or so; a few inches under six foot. His brown hair was curly, cut short. His eyes brown in a roundish, handsome face. The eyes were staring past Hart at the back of the room. At the man with the grey three-piece suit and wire-framed spectacles. At Lacy.

They were eyes brimming with hatred so strong that Hart could read it clearly from the middle of the room. There was a gun holstered at his side that looked about to carry the message. Hart watched as the younger man's hand moved until it was only inches above the pistol butt.

He stepped a foot away from the bar and his voice was clear and loud: "Lacy!"

The way Lacy slowly turned his head in the direction of the door, Hart thought maybe he'd known the youngster was there all along. Either that, or he was cool as ice.

"You killed 'em, Lacy. My brothers. Killed 'em or had 'em killed. I been waitin' for you to come out of that place you keep stashed up in an' show yourself. An' now you done it."

He moved his head to one side and back again.

"Now I'm goin' to kill you."

Lacy turned his body in the chair and stared along the room. Then he carefully removed his spectacles, folded them and slipped them back down into his pocket.

"I don't know what you're talking about, Waterford."

He spoke quietly but in the silence that now held the saloon every word was clear.

Dan Waterford flushed. "You're a liar. You had 'em killed. Both of 'em. Shot down like they was animals, worse than that, trash."

"I still don't know what you're talking about. I'm sorry." Lacy nodded his head and turned away, picking up his glass and drinking the whisky slowly.

Dan Waterford cursed and walked half a dozen yards into the room. Hart saw the hand curved above the gun and noticed that it was trembling from a mixture of excitement and fear. He looked into Waterford's eyes and tried to figure out which was the strongest. He settled for the last. He doubted if Waterford had ever shot a man before; if he'd ever drawn on a man either.

Hart remembered the bulge in Lacy's coat and knew that the youngster was about to get himself killed if he pressed things too far.

"Lacy! You cowardly, lying, bastard!"

Someone jumped up from the table but

it wasn't Lacy. The bearded man's face was red with anger, his voice louder than ever. "Shut that Irish mouth of yours and get the hell out of here while you can still walk!"

"Henry, you keep out of this!"

"Don't you tell me what I can do, boy. I don't need advice from the likes of you."

Waterford's hand dropped closer to his gun. His face went white. "What's that mean?"

The big man unbuttoned his coat, revealing a wide gunbelt. "It means that if your brothers were killed like trash that's because trash is what they was."

Dan Waterford's fingers grabbed for the butt of his gun; Henry's hand went under the flap of the coat, reaching for his own weapon. Wes Hart was faster than both of them. Before either man could clear leather, he'd sprung to his feet and his arm had moved through a blurring arc which brought the Colt out of the holster and finished with it rock steady in his hand, hammer cocked and ready.

Waterford saw: hesitated.

Hart's eyes told him, don't do it, don't go through with it.

Waterford sucked in the right side of his mouth and carried on pulling the gun clear. Hart jumped forward, bringing his right arm up and round. The side of the Colt's barrel smashed against the youngster's head and he slumped backwards, mouth open in a shout. As he rocked back against the bar, his hand dropped clear of his pistol. He leaned for a few moments against the counter, a line of blood running through his brown hair and down his cheek.

Henry's pistol was in his hand, the arm angled towards the floor, surprise startling his bearded face. Lacy was staring at Hart with renewed interest and Hart noticed that his right hand was close by the lapel of his suit.

"I ought to finish that no-good bastard right now!"

Henry began to bring up the gun, but one look from Hart was enough to make him stop.

"He's been drinkin'," said Hart, stepping between the youngster and the two men at the back of the room. "He ain't goin' to do you any harm now."

Henry still hesitated: Lacy continued to watch, playing no part.

"You got a lawman in town?" Hart asked.

"Not right now."

"Okay."

Hart released the hammer on the Colt and slid it down into his holster. He turned towards Waterford and scooped him up with one arm, setting him over one shoulder. "I'll get him outside in the air. Let him sober up."

Bearing Dan Waterford as if he were little more than a child, Hart left the saloon.

Jake Henry stood open-mouthed. "Who in hell's name was that?"

Lacy arched his fingers, pressing the tips lightly together. "I don't know," he said quietly. "I don't know but I think we're going to find out."

6

HART forked another mouthful of beans up from his plate, the sauce dripping down thickly. He broke off a chunk of corn bread and wiped it around one half of the plate, mopping up bean juice, egg yolk and bacon fat and pushing it into his mouth. He chewed a while, swallowed and drank some coffee, black and bitter. The bed hadn't been too good, the straw mattress lumpy and torn and set on wooden boards, but at least the breakfast was making up for it.

He stretched and belched—the four other boarders glanced round at him and quickly looked away again. Hart grinned and pushed his fork into the beans. They were midway to his mouth when the door opened and Lacy stepped inside.

The fork dropped from Hart's hand with a clatter, splashing yellow-brown juice over the table and the front of his shirt. Hart's hand was at the edge of the table, close to his holster.

Lacy stood quite still, waiting for those who'd turned round to get back to their own breakfasts and business. Then he pointed to the chair opposite where Hart was sitting.

"I'd like to join you."

Hart nodded. "Sure."

Lacy pulled out the chair and sat down carefully, as if he was afraid of creasing his suit.

"Coffee?"

"Thank you, no."

"You don't mind if I . . ." Hart looked at his plate.

"Go right ahead."

Hart finished his breakfast, thinking about what Lacy had come for; thinking that he could guess but that with a man like Lacy it didn't pay to be too sure until you knew.

He wiped at his mouth with the back of his hand and eased his chair away from the table.

"What's on your mind?"

Lacy's mouth moved fractionally in what might have been the beginnings of a smile—it probably wasn't.

"You were impressive last night."

Hart looked at his face, saying nothing. The light blue eyes refused to flicker.

"But, then," Lacy continued, "I presume that was your intention."

"Go on."

"You're new in town, you wear a gun as though you can use it, you're probably looking for work. What better way to get it than by showing your worth."

Hart drained his cup of coffee. "Who was I showin' it to?"

Lacy took out his spectacles and put them on. The woman who ran the boarding-house came over and asked him if there was anything he wanted. Lacy said there wasn't.

To Hart he said: "The man you stopped going for his gun was Jake Henry. He manages the Beaumont mine. The one you pistol-whipped is called Dan Waterford. He isn't anything."

"Like his brothers?" Hart asked.

"As I said in the saloon, I know nothing about Waterford's brothers."

"But they might have been killed?"

Lacy sighed lightly and sat back in the chair. "Of course they might. Tago's an unruly place. Men argue, fight, get knifed or shot and nobody knows why or cares. What might have happened to that boy's brothers is no concern of mine."

"Yeah."

"What did you do with him last night?"

"Dumped his head in the horse trough, then left him propped up against the wall."

Lacy set his finger-tips together. "And was I correct that you are looking for work?"

"The right kind. Maybe."

"Would something along the lines of last evening's play in the saloon be along those lines?"

"It might."

Lacy sighed again. "You're an unduly evasive man, Mr . . ."

Hart let the search for his name hang. "You ain't made your proposition yet."

"Very well. Tago needs a lawman, a marshal, regulator, call it what you will. We sent for one, a gunman named Hart. Have you heard of him?"

Hart nodded. "I reckon."

"He hasn't showed. If you want the job, it's yours."

"Regulator."

"Yes."

"What does it pay?"

"Hundred a month and all round."

Hart shook his head.

"A hundred and twenty-five. That's the top offer. It's already too much."

Hart shook his head again and stood up. "Sorry."

Lacy removed his spectacles. "A hundred and fifty."

Hart stood away from the table. "Who'll I be workin' for? You?"

"Not precisely."

"Then who? Precisely."

"Mason Beaumont."

"Fine. I'll talk to Beaumont."

Lacy eased back his chair and stood up, facing Hart. He was shorter by an inch, thinner and lighter by some forty pounds.

"It isn't necessary."

"That's where you're wrong. I talk to the man who's payin' me or I don't work."

Lacy turned half away, considering. After a few moments he looked back. His face was showing something now—it showed that he was being pushed and he didn't like it.

"The Beaumont place is north-west of town. Almost a mile. You can't miss it. Mr. Beaumont will see you at eleven." He stared at Hart pointedly. "You might clean up before then."

Lacy had been right when he'd said the Beaumont house couldn't be missed. It stood at the end of a long avenue of aspens, its white painted boards gleaming in the bright sunlight.

Hart led the grey on to the gravel drive and rode slowly towards the house. It was two storeys high, a steep angled roof leading to brick chimneys at either end. The windows were covered with white shutters, all save one of which were closed across. Rounded wooden pillars supported an arched roof over the veranda that ran along two-thirds of the house front. The main door was set behind the arch. Wisteria climbed up frames attached both to verandas and walls, lavender with occasional flowers of pink, rose or white.

A rocker stood empty on the porch. There was no sign of anyone around. Hart reined in the mare and waited. He pushed back the brim of his hat, warm in the sun. He was wearing a grey cotton shirt and black pants pushed down into brown boots, a leather vest unbuttoned over the shirt.

After a few moments a man came around the corner of the house, a Negro. He was older than Charlie, older and darker, his hair greying and his back stooped more than a little.

"Yes, sir?"

Hart made a face. "Don't sir me, just tell Beaumont I'm here to see him."

"Yes, sir. Who shall I tell him it is, sir?"

"Don't call . . ." Hart realized it wasn't worth it. "Just tell him his regulator's here."

The Negro put his head over to one side, as if he hadn't heard quite correctly.

"Regulator?"

"Yeah, you heard it right."

"Yes, sir." The black turned away and climbed the steps towards the house. He was met by Lacy coming out.

"You got here, then," he said to Hart, taking the watch from his vest pocket and clicking it open to check the time.

"Yeah, an' clean, too."

Hart dismounted and tied the reins to the rails in front of the veranda.

"Mr. Beaumont's waiting to speak with you. On your insistence."

"Sure."

Hart walked past Lacy towards the door; this time it was the Negro who was coming out.

"Mr. Beaumont says—" he began.

"Uh-huh," grunted Hart, moving past him.

"You can get back to your work," said Lacy stiffly, following Hart into the hallway.

The inside of the house smelt of flowers; they were everywhere, in vases that were tall and small, thin and round. White and pink blossoms, blue and red and yellow.

The boards of the floor were so polished that if you looked down it was possible to see a blurred reflection.

"Upstairs," said Lacy.

The staircase wound round to the upper floor. On the landing Lacy went past Hart and stopped by the furthest door.

"This is Mr. Beaumont's room."

Hart nodded. "Whose are the others?"

Lacy gave him a look of contempt and turned the handle. Inside the room the atmosphere was different. There was a scent that might have been of flowers, but if so they were dying, decaying. To Hart the room smelt of death, sickly sweet like rotting flesh.

He looked at the portrait of the Confederate major on the wall and then, only then, at the man in the white suit sitting in the leather chair beneath it.

"Mr. Beaumont?"

The short man looked at Hart, then past him to where Lacy was standing in the doorway. "All right, Lacy. I'll call you if there's anything."

"Mr. Beaumont, I—"

The podgy hand waved and Lacy stopped in mid sentence, abruptly quitting the room. His footsteps sounded down the corridor.

"You come with high recommendation," said Beaumont. "Lacy isn't a man who's impressed easily."

"I'll bet."

Beaumont waved a hand towards a glass-fronted cupboard at the side of the room. "A drink?"

"No, thanks."

"Then fetch one for me. There's a decanter of brandy over there."

Hart hesitated, not liking the man's assumption that he was going to be waited on; irritated, also, by the high pitch of his voice. But he shrugged and poured the brandy.

The air was stifling; when he came close to Beaumont to hand him the glass Hart could smell the sweat of the man's body. He glanced at the windows and saw that the shutters were closed against two of the three windows.

"Lacy has told you my terms?"

"Yeah, a hundred and fifty a month and all found. Board, an' ammunition. What wants doin'?"

Mason Beaumont gulped at the large glass of brandy. "There's a lot of money in Tago. Money being dragged and blown out of those hills as silver. Most of it's mine. Tago is mine. This house is mine. I don't want to see any of them threatened. I want them to grow." He swallowed some more brandy. "Grow around me."

"And?"

"The town needs a firm hand. Control."

"How 'bout Lacy?"

Beaumont touched one corner of his fleshy mouth. "Lacy is my, er, companion. I don't want him getting involved in that mess,"

"But it's okay for me?"

"At a hundred and fifty dollars, yes."

"So you just want the placed cleaned up? Settled down."

Beaumont wriggled a little in his chair. "There's more to it than that."

Hart nodded. "I figured there would be."

Beaumont's small dark eyes looked past Hart towards the door. He beckoned him closer and leaned forward. "Someone is doing their best to ruin me." The eyes blinked. "Totally."

Hart waited for him to continue. When he did the voice was thinner and quieter than before.

"For the past three months there have been raids on the mine, on the assay office, on shipments going from here east.

Whoever is behind it knows too much about my business. I don't . . ." He glanced again at the door. "I don't trust anyone."

Hart straightened up "Not even your companion?"

Beaumont bristled and downed the rest of his glass. "Get me another brandy!"

Hart grinned and did so; this time he helped himself too.

"You got anyone else workin' for you?" Hart asked. "Outside of Lacy and the people at the mine. Anyone who might handle a gun, I mean?"

"There's a man named Carter. Two others called . . ."

Hart finished it for him. "Noonan and Moody."

The fresh glass of brandy slipped between Beaumont's fingers, splashing over his lap. The glass rolled along his leg and fell to the floor, splintering apart. Both men held their breath, waiting for Lacy to walk through the door.

But nothing happened.

Mason Beaumont's face was screwed

into a white mask. "Who *are* you? What did Lacy say your name was?"

Hart smiled with his eyes. "Lacy didn't say. Lacy didn't know."

Beaumont closed his eyes, wiping a hand across his forehead. It came away wet with sweat.

"Who . . . ?"

"The name's Hart. Wes Hart."

Beaumont shook. "You . . . you said you weren't coming. Wouldn't . . . , didn't want the job."

"And that was when you sent Crazy John Carter back after me."

The hardness of Hart's voice drove Beaumont back into the leather chair. He looked around wildly for a way out but Hart seemed to be filling all the space before him.

"What happened to . . . to Carter and . . . the others?"

The faded blue of Hart's eyes bore into Beaumont. "Same as I guess you intended for me. I killed 'em."

Mason Beaumont turned his head and jammed his fist to his mouth, but he was too late to stop the thin trail of vomit springing from between his purple lips. Hart stared with disgust as it ran along his arm, dripping from his thick, round fingers to the white leather of the chair and the carpeted floor.

When he looked at Hart again his eyes were misted, glazed with what might have been tears.

"What are . . . ?" He couldn't bring himself to finish the question.

Hart let his right hand drop to his boot and when it came up the Apache knife was tight within it. Beaumont stared at it transfixed.

"A second," said Hart softly. "That's all it would take to slit your fat throat from ear to ear."

Beaumont's mouth fell open, thin lines of spittle hanging past his chin.

"But seein' as you wanted me to work for you so bad . . . enough to have me killed when I said no . . . I figured maybe it might be a job worth takin'."

A blob of perspiration balanced on the

end of Beaumont's nose, then fell. He gulped: "You want to take . . . the job?"

Hart nodded: "Uh-huh."

"I don't . . ."

"I'm not sure I do."

Hart saw Beaumont's eyes move fractionally towards the door. Lacy hadn't been there before—that didn't mean he hadn't come back.

"You did say," said Hart quietly, "you didn't trust anybody?"

Beaumont's white face nodded.

"That's fine. 'Cause I feel the same way. I'd hate for you to set anyone else on to me. Lacy, for instance."

Beaumont's head shook from side to side, his eyes promising that he wouldn't think of doing anything like that.

"See, if you did . . . after killing him, then I'd have to come and kill you."

The point of the knife moved closer to Mason Beaumont's throat and Beaumont's eyes jerked shut, his head pushed back against the leather of the chair. He shook.

Hart withdrew the knife and slipped it

back into the sheath inside his boot; he stepped soundlessly to the door. The first Beaumont realized he'd gone was when he heard the door closing.

Beaumont sat in the chair, mouth open, thinking of the small violet bottle in the cabinet; trying not to think of the wet stain that was darkening the front of his white trousers.

7

WES HART moved his room at the Widdens' boarding-house from the small upstairs back to the larger upstairs front. The bed was bigger and had springs under a mattress that was stuffed with more than straw. From the window he could see along Silver Street right into the main square. Looking straight across he had a good view of the shell of the church that was being put up to the east of the town and if he swivelled his head he saw the tents down towards the river.

Not far along Silver Street was the livery barn where Hart had installed the dapple grey, making sure the owner understood just how important it was that she be properly cared for.

The store immediately past the livery had provided boxes of cartridges for his Colt Peacemaker and for the Henry that was his saddle gun—also 10-gauge shot for the sawn-off Remington. He'd bought a new blue cotton shirt, some thick socks to wear inside his boots and several other things that had taken his fancy.

The store had been more than reasonable when Hart had explained that the payment would be made when he received his wages from Mason Beaumont. Since Beaumont owned the store anyway, it didn't seem to matter a great deal. And if it had, the look in the stranger's faded blue eyes and the way he hefted the shotgun would have driven such thoughts from the manager's mind.

So far all Hart had done was to walk around the town a few times, getting to know the place. He couldn't be certain that Beaumont had taken his warning to heart and if anyone was being sent after him then he preferred to be out in the open where he could see them coming.

But nothing happened. He didn't see Lacy, nor anyone else who looked suspicious. Not that that made him drop his guard.

Hart discovered that the Silver Star wasn't the only saloon that Tago possessed. There were three others close to the square, each one smaller and more squalid than the last. He passed a barber's shop and an undertaker's; two stores selling mostly mining supplies; another place selling boots and clothing; a saddler's, a couple more general stores, a butcher's and an apothecary's. There were five eating houses, two laundries and one brothel.

It wasn't a whole lot different from any other mining town.

In the daytime the place seemed pretty deserted, with most of the men and children up on the hills either side of the river searching for silver ore. Some folk would stay up there for weeks at a time, living in makeshift shacks; others would drift back down into town every opportunity they got. For those of them who'd struck lucky there was little enough in Tago to take it away from them, but they still did their best to spend it. Apart from Beaumont's saloon and stores, there were other places, other people anxious to help those who had money to get rid of it. Small-time grafters and gamblers swarmed round the place like blue flies, fattening as fast as they could. The saloon girls and the hustlers and the whores from the brothel scarcely had time to pull their under-things back on between trips.

In the daytime it was women and broken men and boys too young and weak to help shift rock; it was wagons carrying in supplies and lines of mules and every now and again a man riding through with a haunted look in his eye and a pistol hung low from his hip. When darkness began to fall it was different: the men were drinking hard or already drunk; the gamblers were hunched over their cards praying for the next deal to bring them the straight flush that life had denied; the women were painted and brazen, their eyes staring boldly into men's faces counting the money they saw there; the wives sat alone listening to the turn and cry of the kids and twisting their fingers hard in their laps until they hurt.

Hart had walked round Tago in the light and nothing had happened: now he was stepping out into the dark.

He drew the Colt easily from its holster and spun the chamber against the palm of his left hand, hearing the rolling click and sliding the gun back down into the greased leather. He secured the thong about his leg, leaving the one which held the hammer free. He picked up the sawn-off Remington and broke the fourteen-inch barrels, checking the load. The weapon snapped back with a loud metallic crack.

Hart set the shotgun on the bed while he unfolded the Indian blanket and draped it over his left shoulder. He picked up the shotgun with his left hand, concealing it under the coloured patterns of the blanket.

He had his leather vest on over his new blue shirt; grey pants outside worn boots, worn and easy. Hart scooped up his flat-crowned black hat and fixed it on his head, angling the front downwards so that it almost shielded his eyes.

He touched the palm of his right hand once again, momentarily, to the butt of his Colt then left the room. Down the stairs and out into the street.

It was passing from dusk to night. The air was thickening and cold. Lights glowed muzzily. The sound of voices drifted from the square. Hart walked out into the middle of Silver Street and set off towards the source of the noise, stepping purposefully.

There was a wagon hitched up outside the Silver Star and on either side of it some dozen horses. More were tethered at points round the square. A shadow moved on the edge of the boardwalk and instantly Hart halted, his body dipped, hand hovering over his gun.

The shadow became a shape, became a man. Medium height, wearing a grubby stetson and a wool coat. He stared at Hart and shook his head, uncertainly. Then he carried on towards the saloon doors.

Hart straightened and followed him. Over the top of the still swinging doors he could see most of the long room. The same bartender was behind the same greasy counter, only this time he had two others helping him out. A line of men stood facing them, glasses by their hands. Around half of the tables were occupied, some playing cards, others just talking, drinking. The red-head he'd seen on the balcony the day he'd arrived was standing on the stairs to the left of the room, one arm snaked round the bannister.

Hart pushed the doors open and went in; he paused for a moment before pushing his way to the bar. The barkeep recognized him and came forward.

"Whisky."

"Sure."

Men who'd been there when Hart had dealt with Dan Waterford, others who'd only heard about it, began looking at Hart, pointing, talking. The man next to him, a rangy miner with dirt engrained into face and hands, offered to shake his hand and buy him a drink. A bearded man to the other side spat down at the floor and cursed him for not letting the

Irishman go ahead and kill Jake Henry when he had the chance.

Hart half-turned, his face cold with controlled anger. "Maybe I'd've left him to it if I'd thought the kid had any kind of chance. As it stood the only thing he was goin' to get for himself was a couple of slugs in the chest."

The bearded man looked up at Hart with a scowl. "An' now?"

"Now I got a job to do. Now I'd've stopped it no matter who was goin' to get shot."

The man moved back a few feet along the bar, elbowing someone else out of the way. "A job? What the hell kind of job is that?"

"Regulator."

The bearded man's tongue showed for a moment between his lips and he blinked. "You don't say. Beaumont's regulator, eh?"

The line of Hart's mouth tightened. "That was what I *didn't* say. I don't belong to Beaumont, nor anyone else."

"Yeah? Who the hell pays your wages?"

"That don't mean he owns me."

The man barely turned his head before spitting. "Shit! Mason Beaumont owns this town and everythin' in it." He stared at Hart pointedly. "Everyone!"

Hart took half a pace back, as if moving away. Then he swung his right arm, fist bunched, leaning all the weight of his body behind the punch. The fist struck the bearded man on the side of the jaw and jolted him back hard, slamming him into the pair behind. There were shouts and curses and then the sound of Hart's fist hammering home again into the man's face. Bone gave under the force of the blow and the crunch was accompanied by a jet of blood from the man's broken nose.

Several others jumped wide, throwing their glasses down, some starting to reach for the guns at their hips.

Hart spun so that his back was to the bar and his hand moved in a blurring movement that only stopped when the

Colt .45 was steady and raised, hammer cocked.

"Jesus Christ!"

Everyone close stopped as if frozen. Further back into the saloon conversations continued, fading now as heads turned round realizing what was going down.

The bearded man rolled over on the floor until his body pressed against the foot of the bar. He was covered in spilt beer and spit and his own blood. One arm was cradled about his head.

Five others stood watching Hart, fear clear and easy in their eyes.

A glass tinkled—a laugh caught and broke: the saloon was still.

Hart ran his eyes around the room, making sure that he saw everyone, that everyone saw him.

When he spoke his voice was taut like steel.

"I'll say this once an' I hope I don't have to spell it out again. I don't want to have to beat it into every one of you, but I will if I have to. I'm Wes Hart. I'm regulator here in Tago. Since now. That means I'm keepin' the law. But I ain't doin' it with no badge. I'm doin' it with this—" he lifted the Colt Peacemaker so that everyone could see "— that's my law."

Hart paused, letting his words sink in.

"One more thing—this man here suggested that the law I was keepin' was Beaumont's law." He glanced down. "You can see what happened to him. Sure, Beaumont's payin' my wages, but that's as far as it goes. I run things my way, no one else's."

He looked over the crowd again.

"Any of you doubt that he'd better step out here and say it now."

Nobody moved.

Hart reached round on to the bar and lifted his glass, downing the whisky at a swallow. Slowly he walked towards the doors, men stepping aside to let him pass.

The dog growled and whined at the corner of the alley, hair bristling. Deeper into the darkness something, someone, moved. Hart stepped back out of the light.

He heard footsteps, unsteady; a voice, low and unclear. Towards the end of the street, two men appeared, riding their horses slowly towards where Hart was standing. In the alley, the dog growled louder and began to bark. The man swung his foot at it and missed, cursing. The dog snapped at his heels and he kicked again, the thump of boot on flesh testifying to his success. As the dog ran off into the shadow, the man saw Hart for the first time.

Swaying slightly, he looked at him, not able to get his face into focus. The two riders came closer. Finally the man gave up the attempt and lurched towards the door of the small saloon.

The two men reined in their mounts and dismounted. Hart followed them through the door. The interior was thick with smoke and loud with voices braying and talking. A few leaned round at the tables and glanced at Hart, but not too many paid him much attention. It wasn't the kind of place where it paid to stare at a man for too long.

"Whisky."

The bartender sniffed and wiped the edge of his hand under his nose before reaching for the bottle; wiped the hand down his vest before picking up a glass. The men who'd come in ahead of Hart were talking to a group of miners further along the bar.

The light from three hurricane lamps positioned down the centre of the room sent some men into sharp relief and left others in shadow.

"Seen you around?" asked the bartender.

"No."

"Thought not." He sniffed a few more times and moved away to serve someone else.

Hart tried the whisky and it was as sharp and sour as he'd thought it would be. When he put the glass down he realized that one of the group of men along the bar was saying something about him and pointing at the blanket draped over Hart's left shoulder.

Hart waited, knowing the man would allow himself to be encouraged by his companions and would grow louder as he went on.

"What's the matter, stranger? White man's clothes not good enough for you?"

He was young, maybe a couple of years over twenty, his face already flushed with drink. A black leather gunbelt was buckled at his hips and a pistol hung low in the holster. Dark, curly hair showed under the brim of his hat; his eyes shifted as he spoke.

"Hear me? You hear me?"

Hart stood away from the bar. "I hear you."

The two who'd come in ahead of Hart were at the kid's right, a few paces behind him. One of them was an older man, lines carved into his face and etched out by the shadow and line of the light. A pistol was tucked down into his belt, angling across his body. His companion was around thirty, clean shaven, a gun holstered for a left-hand draw.

There were three more to the bar side and Hart counted three more weapons.

"I asked if you was an Indian lover?"

"An' I heard."

"So how come you ain't answerin'?" The kid curled his lip.

Hart said it loud and clear so that almost everyone in the saloon could hear. "I don't talk to drunks. Specially drunken kids."

The lip curled again into a snarl; the youngster's hand was closer to his gun butt; he was breathing through his open mouth, loudly.

"Mister, you're goin' to regret that."

"I doubt it."

Only one man continued to talk, somewhere towards the far side of the smoky room. Everyone else was waiting, watching, a few standing on tables to get a better view.

"You damned Indian-lovin' bas—"

The kid went for his gun and as he did so Hart brought up his left arm, jerking the blanket clear. Suddenly, his fingers beginning to tighten around the butt of his pistol, the kid was staring down the barrels of a sawn-off shotgun.

His mouth fell open, jaw slackened; breath came harshly as his hand jerked away from his gun. The older man's face frowned with surprise and his own movement towards the pistol angled into his belt stopped short. None of the others moved, spoke. They were too intent upon the shotgun and the man standing behind it.

"Okay, boy, you got some apologizin' to do."

The youngster struggled for words but they stuck in his throat; he couldn't drag his eyes away from the way Hart's finger was curled inside the trigger guard. He knew that it would only need the merest movement to blast both barrels of shot through his body.

"Now who ain't hearin'?" Hart's voice was the only thing to be heard in the small saloon—apart from the kid's scraping, frightened breath.

"I . . . I."

Hart prodded the shotgun towards him and his eyes closed, face twisting sideways.

"You what? I ain't got all night."

"I'm . . . sorry. Real sorry, mister I never . . . never meant nothin' by it. Honest, I . . ."

"Honest, shit! The only honest thing is that you didn't know I had this Remington stashed away under this blanket an' you'd got yourself enough whisky inside to show off some in front of your friends. Ain't that it, boy? Prove yourself a man? Huh?"

The kid looked away from the gun and down at the soiled floor.

"Yeah." His voice was so soft that it could hardly be heard.

"Louder, boy!"

"Yeah."

Hart stepped forward. "That still ain't loud enough. I want you to shout it out. Sing it!"

The end of the barrels of the shotgun were hard against the youngster's chest and his body was shaking so strongly that it vibrated against the metal.

"Yeah!"

"Yeah, what?"

"Yeah, I was lookin' to show off. Bein' stupid. Stupid drunk."

Hart stepped away and lowered the shotgun. All eyes were still on him, from the light or from the shadow. A few men had begun to talk quietly, whispering about what they'd seen, but as soon as Hart spoke they fell silent.

"I'm the regulator here now. I aim to keep things as law-abidin' as can be." He raised the shotgun again, holding it high. "If I need to use this to do it, then I will."

Hart kept the shotgun where it was and looked slowly around the room. "I hope you all understand that."

He scooped up the blanket and draped it back over his left shoulder, hiding the shotgun from sight. Carefully he backed towards the door, saving his last glance for the kid close by the bar—the youngster quickly turned away. His hand reached towards the whisky glass on the counter and it was shaking like an aspen in the wind.

Hart untied his horse and set his boot inside the stirrup, pulling himself up into the saddle. He'd made himself known enough for one night. Word would travel and travel fast and that was what he wanted. He swung the grey around and set off back to the boarding-house. There was a bottle in his room and he'd pour himself a shot or two before turning in.

At first light he was going to ride up into the hills and take a look around—if he was going to find out who was systematically plundering Beaumont's gold that seemed as good a place to start as any.

8

THE sun was still low in the sky, its brightness hooded by cloud. The wind blew freely from the east, turning the branches of the pines which edged the hill. Below, the water moved a slow, muted blue. Hart reined in the mare and looked down towards the Beaumont mine.

Around the main entrance of the shaft heavy timbers pushed upwards, black and clumsy. A number of men moved about, not in any apparent pattern. There were two long wagons waiting, unloaded past the entrance. Half a dozen mules were tied to a long line; as many horses stood in a rough corral. There was one single-storey building with smoke rising from a hole cut in its roof and three smaller cabins close to its left.

Hart touched the mare's sides with his spurs and set her into a walk. The top surface of the ground was firm and ridged and where hoofmarks broke it through they exposed a darker, softer soil underneath.

He was eighty yards away from the mine when a shout made him turn, reining in.

"Where you headin', mister?"

The man was on a curved ledge of rock to Hart's right, the sun coming up over his shoulder so that his head and shoulders appeared in silhouette. He might be good and keeping quiet and out of sight but he was presenting too easy a target of himself.

Hart saw the rifle raised to the man's shoulder; took his time before answering. "Just goin' into the mine. Lookin' around."

"We don't take to no visitors."

Hart still couldn't make out the features of the man's face, only the outline.

"You tell Jake Henry I'm here. Wes Hart. He'll clear me."

The man shook his head quickly. "I

can't do that. You ain't got no proper business, you ride back."

"Ride in an' ask him." An edge of temper was beginning to show underneath the flat tone of Hart's voice.

"I can't leave my post."

"Then we're stuck here all morning, cause I ain't turnin' round. Not now."

The rifle was pulled into the shoulder. Hart touched the tip of his tongue to his dry lips. He freed his boots from the stirrups, ready to throw himself from the saddle.

The sound of voices rose from the mine. Hart glanced round to see three men leading mounts from the corral.

"Guess we're gettin' company," he said.

The man on the rock didn't reply; waited. Hart picked out Jake Henry right off, riding in the middle of the three and slightly ahead. A Winchester lay across the front of his saddle, held fast.

Henry acknowledged Hart with a nod and called to the guard. "What's up?"

The man pointed his rifle. "He come

by sayin' he was ridin' down to the mine. Didn't know him so I told him he wasn't."

Jake Henry moved his horse nearer to Hart. His bearded face scowled. "Seems to me your business is back down in town. That was what you was hired for. Up here I handle things an' I don't need no regulator to help me do it."

The face reddened as the harsh voice grew louder.

Hart looked at the mine manager evenly. "You listen to me. First off, I don't recall you bein' around when I was hired so I don't see how you know more about what I'm supposed to be doin' than I do myself. Then again, what I hear, handlin' things up here is where you're fallin' down on your ass."

Jake Henry turned his horse away, then pulled it back. His eyes blazed dangerously and the rifle was no longer across his saddle, but by his side. The two miners who'd ridden up with him had their hands close by the pistols at their belts.

"You sure do believe in takin' risks!"

Hart shook his head. "Uh-uh. You ain't plannin' to do anythin' foolish, are you? Besides, like I say, I just rode up to talk. Nothin' to get steamed up about . . . not unless there are things you got reason not to want to talk about."

"What the hell does that mean?"

Hart shrugged, enjoying the man's evident discomfort. "Means what it says. That's all." He glanced up at the guard on the rock, whose rifle was now lowered to his hip. "We goin' to hang around up here all mornin' or can we ride down and talk proper?"

Henry nodded and pulled on the rein. "Let's go."

He rode ahead, driving the horse harder than was necessary, taking his temper out with each kick of his boots and slap of the reins. Hart rode easily behind, taking his own time. Something was biting at Jake Henry and he didn't think it was just what had been said, nor his memory of the other night. There had to be more to it than that.

Henry waited for him outside the long shack. "Come on in," he said grudgingly.

The building was divided into two and this half was evidently Henry's office. A desk angled out from the back wall; piles of papers, assayer's reports and the like covered most of its surface. Over to the side an iron stove burned, smoke going up through a badly joined pipe leading to the roof. Two maps and a drawing of the interior of the mine were fastened to the left-hand wall. More papers stood in heaps on the floor.

Jake Henry leaned his rifle against the desk and pulled back a chair. He pointed over towards a second chair and sat down himself. Hart preferred to remain standing.

"You're a mighty pushy man," said Henry. "It ain't good."

"Maybe I'm the best judge of that."

Henry drew in one side of his face, started to reply, changed his mind, said something else instead. "What was the meanin' of that remark about me not bein' able to handle things up here?"

Hart shrugged and set one foot on the seat of the chair. "Maybe nothin' much . . . just somethin' Beaumont said."

Henry flushed and pressed both hands down on the arms of his chair. "What did that sneaky bastard say?"

Hart allowed himself a thin smile. "That ain't no way to talk 'bout your employer."

One of Henry's hands bunched and hammered down on to the desk top, shifting some of the papers sideways. "What did the bastard say?"

"Just about the trouble you been havin' keepin' much of the silver you been diggin' out. Seems as soon as you got it out the rock someone comes along and says thanks very much an' takes it for his own. Beaumont seemed awful tired of that."

Henry stood up and glared across the room at Hart. "None of that's my responsibility. I'm paid to make sure the silver's mined efficiently and that's all."

Hart paused a few seconds before speaking, his voice quiet and almost hiding his sarcasm. "Then it's a shame Beaumont don't see it that way."

Jake Henry kicked at the leg of the desk, and stepped past it. A sheaf of papers began sliding towards the floor, slowly, a few at a time. Henry reached into his pocket and pulled out a silver flask. He unscrewed the cap and set the flask to his mouth, swallowing quickly.

"You arrange shipments, don't you? Ore shipments."

"Of course, that's—" Henry stopped abruptly, eyes widening. "Are you . . . ?"

"I'm not sayin' nothin'. Just askin' questions. Gettin' a few things clear."

"If you think I had anything to do with—"

Hart stopped him with a gesture of his outstretched hand. "Take it easy. I said, all I want is information."

Jake Henry was sweating. He took another swig from his flask and walked towards the window, trying to calm himself down.

Hart waited a few moments, taking his

foot from the chair and going towards the stove.

"From what Beaumont said, whoever's been raiding these shipments had a pretty good idea of when they were being made."

Henry turned from the window. "That's nothing. Nothing. A lot of people could know that. In a place like this, a lot of men working, it's difficult to keep things like that secret."

Hart said nothing: stared.

"What the hell does Beaumont want from me?"

"Ask him."

"Jesus!"

Jake Henry turned his face to one side, momentarily closing his eyes. Someone knocked at the door and opened it without waiting for an answer. Henry blistered into him and the door closed fast.

"You don't have any ideas, then?"

"About what?"

"Who might be behind these silver robberies."

"I told you—no!" Henry's voice was a loud rasp. He glared at Hart hard before going back to his desk. "Is that all you wanted?"

"Maybe." Hart looked at the manager keenly, ursettling him still further. "It'll do for now."

Henry unbuttoned his coat, easing the flap back over his holster with his arm. "If you've got ideas of coming back and snoopin' around, forget 'em."

"You got secrets, Henry?"

"I got a job to do. You saw that guard up there with a rifle. Next time there'll be more of them—and they'll have orders to shoot first and ask after."

Hart shook his head in a half-smile. "Henry, you're actin' plenty strange for a man who's only doin' a job."

The bearded man let his hand fall nearer to his pistol. Hart moved in fast, his face less than an arm's length away. "You're wastin' your breath threatenin' me an' after the other night you should know it. I've got a job to do too an' if you get in my way I'll knock you aside without thinkin' on it. You understand that?"

The blue eyes stared hard at Henry, continuing until the manager looked away, down at the jumble of papers on his desk.

"Be seein' you."

Hart backed to the door, opened it and stepped outside. Jake Henry made no attempt to move. Only when he heard Hart's horse going away did he unscrew the top of the flask and swallow some more brandy.

Dan Waterford stood below the crest of the hill, the cabin that he and his brothers had built together further down to his right. Yards in front of him were their graves. Jimmy and Frank. Wooden markers leaned backwards behind heaps of rounded earth. The names had been scratched into the wood with the point of Dan's knife. The knife his father had given him one winter's night, not long before his body was hauled out of the water, dead. "You take it, son," he'd said. "It's sharp, strong. Use it well."

Dan shook his head and stared at the names etched on to the markers. He had used it well enough. *Jimmy Waterford. Frank Waterford*. Tall, slanting letters. The only one of the family who'd ever really learned to write. Hour after hour in the kitchen, his mother fussing and prodding and leaving him every few minutes to look at the stew bubbling on the stove —half of it vegetables that had been left rotting at the market—or the bread rising alongside it.

Underneath each name the same legend —*murdered in cold blood*.

Dan didn't know for certain which of Beaumont's men had done it, but he was certain that was who it had been. They'd been snapping at their heels ever since the brothers had arrived as if Tago wasn't big enough for all comers. That day Jimmy and Frank had been gunned down, the manager of Beaumont's bank had refused him another loan. And when he'd ridden back to break the news . . .

He didn't know whose word it had been—Jake Henry or Lacy—but whoever it was they were as good as dead. He vowed it.

Dan Waterford closed his eyes and his hands automatically joined before his chest. His lips began to move but the words wouldn't come; words of a prayer he'd known by heart since childhood. Words of any prayer. He couldn't pray while it weighed down on him the way it did.

Tears formed behind his eyes and he turned his head aside. Soon, he said to himself, soon, and then you can rest.

The sound of a rider approaching broke his thoughts. He looked quickly up towards the hill and then broke into a run, heading down towards the cabin. Whoever it might be, he wasn't taking any chances. His boots slithered on the uneven surface and twice he had to steady himself with a hand pushed down against the ground.

Hastily he threw open the door and jumped inside. There was a rifle alongside the fireplace and he grabbed at it, working the lever and hurrying to the window. He eased the sacking aside and waited, watching the crest of the hill.

The fact that he'd only heard a single rider made him easier, though until he saw who it was there was no taking chances. Jake Henry wouldn't let the other evening's business in the Silver Star rest, Dan was certain of that. And probably Lacy wouldn't either.

But it was neither man who rode into sight. Instead it was the tall figure of the man who'd knocked him down in the saloon, his black hat outlined for a moment against the light blue of the sky before horse and rider began to move down the hill.

Waterford's finger began to tighten on the trigger. The man's chest was fast in his sights. The trigger started to move back, fractionally.

Hart saw the barrel of the gun poking past the window edge and threw himself sideways, body bunching as he fell. A shot sang out, the bullet cleaving the air above the grey's saddle. Hart rolled and straightened, hand clawing the Colt from his holster.

"Hold it there!"

"Shit!"

Hart fired at the window, twice, aiming high; he began to run towards the cabin, zig-zagging at first. A second rifle shot tried to find him and missed. Hart fired a third time and gave up any attempt at avoidance. He sprinted hard for the door, crashing into it with his left shoulder and following fast.

Waterford swung the rifle through an arc and Hart barely had time to parry; the barrel struck him high on the left arm and he almost lost his balance, the sudden pain ringing through him.

The younger man tried to use the weapon as a club a second time, but Hart closed fast, ducking under the swing and driving his head into Waterford's chest.

Dan Waterford went back against the wall, trying to kick Hart clear. Hart followed through, punching his left fist into Waterford's stomach and then lifting the Colt. This time he brought the underside of the butt down on to the corner of Waterford's head; it was only a short-swung blow but enough to send him down to the floor.

Hart took half a pace back and cocked the hammer.

Waterford's round face looked up past the gun; his brown eyes were confused but not afraid. Blood showed through a patch of curly, brown hair.

"Why in hell's name am I always pistol-whippin' you?"

Dan Waterford continued to look at him, making no reply.

"'Cause, one time I'm goin' to turn this gun round and use the other end an' you're goin' to end up with more than a little blood lost and an achin' head."

Waterford still didn't say anything, but slowly he looked away. Hart released the hammer of the Colt and stepped further back. He picked up the rifle and ejected the remaining shells on to the floor.

"You always take shots at people ridin' by."

Waterford stood up, rubbing his elbow. "You wasn't ridin' by—you was ridin' in. And besides, there's the business of the other night."

Hart half-smiled. "You take pot shots at a man who saved your life?"

"Did you, hell! I was fixin' to finish that Jake Henry for good."

"Your chances of doin' that were as good as a man who goes fishin' without a line." Hart shook his head. "You couldn't even shoot me when you had a straight chance."

"Yeah."

Waterford wiped at the wetness on his cheek and seemed surprised when he looked at his hand and saw that it was blood.

"You really think one of them killed your brothers?"

"That or had them killed—it don't make a whole lot of difference."

"Maybe it's Beaumont you should be after then. Ain't he back of everything round here?"

"I don't know, he never leaves that

fancy place of his. The way I see it, he leaves most things to Lacy and Henry."

Hart nodded at Waterford's head. "I should see to that cut. Clean it up."

Waterford sighed, nodded, turned away. He swung back fast, his left arm coming up high, bunched fist aiming at Hart's head. Hart leaned back and threw up his own left hand, catching the arm at the wrist. His fingers tightened hard, enough for Waterford to wince.

"I admire a trier, but I wish I knew just what you were tryin' so damned hard for."

"I don't like being shot at and slapped round the head in my own place."

"Then, son, you better make sure next time that when you squeeze the trigger on that Winchester you don't make no mistake. Otherwise you're goin' to end up like them brothers of yours."

Waterford looked for a moment as if he might take another swing with his fist, but instead he went over to the side of the room and poured water from a bucket into a tin bowl and began to wash the blood away from the side of his head.

"You know a gunman name of Carter?" Hart asked, as Waterford was dabbing at his head with a towel.

"Crazy John Carter. Sure. Works for Beaumont. Why, did—"

"Used to."

Waterford turned round, towel by his side. "How d'you mean by that—used to?"

"Last time I saw him he was sprawled all over a store window lookin' pretty dead."

"You killed him, didn't you?"

Hart nodded.

"Then you done folk a favour."

"That was the way I figured it."

"How 'bout Noonan and Moody?"

Hart smiled with his eyes. "They got pretty burned up about it."

Waterford looked at him questioningly, but let it ride. "I reckon on brewin' some tea. You want some?"

"Got any coffee?"

"No."

"Then you go ahead."

When the tea was sitting in a pan at the side of the fire, Hart said, "It wouldn't surprise me if Carter didn't shoot down your brothers. Sounds the sort of thing he'd do."

"I heard he was out of town."

"He could have slipped back. I think he did."

Again Waterford nearly questioned him further, but didn't. He poured the tea into a tin cup, strong smelling and black.

"Even if he did it, he was still followin' orders."

"You don't know that."

"I know how Jake Henry thought of us. You heard what he said down in the saloon." Waterford's eyes narrowed. "I'll kill him sure as I sit here."

Hart nodded. "You know I'm the regulator round here,"

The tea in Waterford's cup slipped over the edge. "Since when?"

"Since yesterday."

Waterford set down the cup. "Does that mean you'll stop me?"

"I did before. If you try to gun Henry down you might have to go past me to do it."

Dan Waterford stood up. "Maybe you should have taken your chance when you had it."

Hart nodded and faced him across the table. "So should you."

He rode back up the hill, pausing only to look for a moment at the inscription on the grave markers. Shaking his head, he flicked at the reins and passed on out of sight of the cabin. He didn't want to kill Dan Waterford—he was trying hard not to—and he hoped the youngster's temper and pride didn't force him into a situation where there was no alternative.

The sun had slid behind a veil of grey clouds and the wind had got up from the east, sharper than before. Hart reached round and freed his Indian blanket from behind the saddle, slipping it round his body. He angled his hat down over his eyes and swung the dapple grey back towards town.

9

IN the week that followed Wes Hart earned his money easy. The show he'd put on that first couple of nights served to keep most of the regulars within bounds and strangers who rode in looking to stir up hell soon got told the new facts of life in Tago. They drank quickly and rode back out, casting furtive glances over their shoulders for the tall regulator with the fast draw and the sawn-off shotgun under the Indian blanket.

Jake Henry sent in a message saying that he was sending a silver shipment east along with four armed guards. Hart met the wagon and rode with it a day's journey out of town. There wasn't any trouble then, nor, as far as they'd heard, for the rest of the trip.

Of Lacy he didn't see anything. Hart presumed he was out at the Beaumont place keeping Mason Beaumont company

—whatever that meant. Everything was as peaceful and law-abiding as a busy mining town could ever be.

It couldn't last.

They were travelling south-west, heading by some roundabout route to California. San Francisco. A party of trappers and grafters who were determined to reach the coast and sign up on board ship. Eight of them in a couple of covered wagons drawn by half a dozen mules all told. They'd set out with two pairs for each wagon but the winter had been long and they'd been out of food and hungry fit to eat any damned thing.

They rolled into Tago, stinking and dirty, patched pants and fur coats, most of them with fur hats as well. A few wore guns, all of them long skinning knives. One man, tall and thin like bent whipcord, carried a long-barrelled Sharps rifle strapped across his back. They drew the wagons up into the yard alongside the livery stable and headed for the nearest saloon to see about getting drunk.

Hart had seen them ride in and nodded

to himself, knowing that nothing in the way of rumour or reputation was ever going to do a thing. He was sitting out on the boardwalk as they went past, enjoying the heat of the sun and stretching his legs. The warmth of the air took the stink of the men and carried it across the street.

Hart sighed and stood up, picking up his hat from the chair back and pushing it down on to his head. Then he walked unhurriedly back to his room to fetch the shotgun.

The saloon the men had picked was the one where Hart had done his blanket and gun trick before—this time he left the blanket behind.

They were already kicking up a din when Hart got to the door. Yelling at the bartender and swallowing down glasses of frothy beer as fast as they could manage. The beer splashed down their faces on to their hide coats and then became puddles on the bare boards of the floor. Perhaps half a dozen others were in the saloon—two drunk, one so fast asleep he would have slept through hell never mind eight men creating a ruckus, three more heading quietly towards the door when Hart stepped fast through it.

"Hold it right there!"

The three who'd been trying to get out gulped, stopped and stared. Those of the eight that heard Hart's words clear spun round. The one nearest to Hart had a Remington .44 tucked down into his belt and as he turned his hand grabbed at the wooden butt. Hart gave him a couple of seconds grace and then made his own draw.

He shot the man through the fleshy part of the upper arm, the impact of the bullet whipping him round and back against the bar, the Remington dropping away in front of him.

Hart lifted his left arm and the double-barrels of the shotgun covered the remainder.

Blood was slowly staining the sleeve of the wounded man's coat, seeping through the thick grease and dirt. More blood dripped to the floor.

"Blast you, feller . . . !" shouted a one-eyed man.

"He shot Vinnie in the arm!"

"Never give him no more chance'n a critter in a trap."

Hart nodded at the three on his left, jerking his head back towards the door. They scuttled through without a word. Over towards the rear of the room, one of the drunks was rubbing his eyes with his arms and trying to work out if it was the whisky working or if it was real.

"When you finished mouthin' off, you can spread yourselves away from the bar." Hart motioned to the left with the shotgun and a couple of the men began to move, the remainder staying put.

The wounded man clutched his shattered arm, face clemmed up with pain. "You didn't have no call to do that," he said through tight lips.

"No? What was you aimin' on doin' with that pistol? Pickin' your nose with it?"

The man scowled, then winced. The fall of blood to the floor quickened.

"That arm of Vinnie's ought to be bound up," complained someone at the end of the bar.

"It'll keep," snapped Hart. "Now do you get away from there and over in front of me or do I have to use another bullet to get some sense into them thick skulls of yours?"

They looked hesitantly at one another but began to move.

"That's it, right across there an' make sure you keep your hands where I can see 'em. Okay. Now, one at a time, from the end, you take out any weapons you got and throw 'em down in front of you."

"In a mule's ass!"

"There ain't no way . . ."

"Fuck yourself, mister!" called one-eye.

The tall, bent man with the Sharps slung over his back chanced a step forward and Hart covered him with the Colt. "I said it afore—you ain't got no right doin' this. We just rode into town lookin' for a drink an'—"

"He ain't no marshal," one of the others interrupted.

"You can get your drink. As much as you like. I'm just fixin' to see no one gets hurt while you're doin' it."

"How 'bout Vinnie?" a man called angrily.

"Vinnie's lucky he didn't stop that slug in his belly an' start in dyin' real slow."

"You mean bastard!"

Hart nodded: "That's right. Now start liftin' them guns an' knives clear. Steady now! One at a time. Anyone moves a finger out of turn an' the only other movin' he's goin' to be doing is up the hill towards the cemetery in the back of a wagon."

The first man fingered out his skinning knife and threw it at the floor. The point stuck into the board and the blade vibrated. A pistol and another, shorter, knife followed it. When it came to his turn, the one-eyed man pointed a scarred hand at Hart. "No man ever took my gun off me before. Knife neither."

"Well, someone's doin' it now."

"That's right," replied the man. "An' I'm goin' to kill him for it. I ain't just goin' to kill him, I'm goin' to skin him alive!"

"I doubt it. Now drop 'em down."

The man did as he was ordered, hatred clear in his face, in the dark pupil of his single eye.

The tall man lowered his head and pulled the Sharps from his back, stepping forward and laying it carefully on the ground.

"I had that rifle a long time," he said. "Don't want nothin' to happen to it." He jerked a finger at Hart. "You understand that? Nothin'."

Hart nodded. "Seems to me you men got a lot of threats for folk who ain't holdin' no cards." He looked over to the bar, where the barkeep was watching carefully. "Come out from there and collect these together. Take 'em over to my place."

While the weapons were being collected, the trappers stared at Hart, waiting for his attention to drift long enough for one of them to charge the space between them. But neither the Colt nor the shotgun faltered.

"Right, let's get this clear. You drink, spend money all you want but you keep out of trouble. When you're ready to move on come an' find me an' you can get your things back. That understood?"

One or two of them nodded.

"Okay."

Hart released the hammer on the Colt and slid it back down into his holster, keeping the men covered with the barrels of the Remington. He pushed his way backwards on to the street, turned and began to walk away.

"Look out!"

The scream of warning in his ears, Hart spun fast, swivelling on the ball of his left foot, right foot off the ground, body folding into a crouch. The shotgun was already in his left hand, fingers of the right hand reaching across to meet it, shortened barrels coming up as the body turned.

The one-eyed trapper was a couple of

feet on to the sidewalk, his right arm high above his head, mid-way through its swing. Light flickered from the thin blade of the knife he'd kept hidden. His mouth was open, his face strained and lean, the single eye fixed on Hart's whirling, steadying body.

Hart squeezed back the triggers of the shotgun.

The blast rocked the air.

The trapper leapt backwards, kicking; the force of the charge took him mostly in the chest. He was hurled backwards against the wall of the saloon, slammed against it so that the boards shook; he rolled sideways, leaving a slanting smear of blood. His right arm and right leg thrust forwards, towards the sidewalk, never quite touching. Before they did, he had toppled down, head meeting the planking with a crack that echoed sharply. He pitched flat, twitched a few times, one arm catching at butterflies in the dying afternoon. Fingers extending, grasping, out and out and out.

Faces in the doorway of the saloon

stared. Across the street the figure of Dan Waterford watched quietly, controlling his breathing, still amazed by the speed and power of what he'd seen.

Men were running along the street towards the sound of the shooting—pulling up short when they could see enough to tell them what had happened—some of them inching closer after that, eager to know more, the manner and horror of dying.

Hart broke the shotgun and pushed fresh loads into place. He pointed towards the doorway. "Out here. Now!"

The seven men trooped into the street, stepping over the slaughtered body of their friend, pausing to look then turning away. Blood dribbled down on to the packed earth of the street from the stained planks of the sidewalk. The front of the trapper's body looked like a field after ploughing and the seed was blood.

"Waterford."

"Yeah?"

"I appreciated your shout. How 'bout one thing more?"

Dan hesitated, uncertain.

"Search 'em. I don't want to turn my back on another stashed weapon."

Waterford nodded and moved into the street. Hart kept the men covered while the youngster ran his hands down their bodies. He pulled out one more knife and nothing more. The bartender from the saloon was waiting at the back of the small crowd that had gathered. Hart sent him back down to fetch the weapons he'd just carried.

"You lost your chance of even a drink. You get your gear together an' ride them wagons back out of town. I'll come a ways with you an' give you your guns an' such. And understand this—any one of you comes back inside Tago I'll shoot him dead without a word."

Hart stared at one man after another, making sure the message sank in. Then he told one of the bystanders to scuttle down to the livery stable and fetch his horse.

A while later he was leaning up against the bar in the Silver Star, buying Dan

Waterford a drink. Evening was settling over the town and the kerosene lamps in the saloon were starting to glow with more brightness. A handful of men were drinking, a couple sitting at a table by the side window over a game of checkers.

"You in town for anythin' special?"

Waterford shook his head.

"Just that I hadn't seen you around for a few days."

"That's right."

Hart took down some of his beer. "What you fixin' to do? You stayin' around and tryin' to work that claim on your own?"

Waterford's brown eyes flicked away. "You know what I'm aimin' to do."

"Still settled on seein' it out with Henry an' Lacy?"

Waterford swallowed down the rest of his beer and set the glass on to the counter, lines of froth sinking down the inside. "You know it."

"An' you know what happened down the street don't make no difference to the way I act."

"Me neither. I figured maybe I owed you that one. Now we're even."

Hart straightened up as the youngster gave him a final look and turned on his heels, heading for the door. For a moment, Hart felt like going after him, trying to calm him down, but he reasoned that it wouldn't do any good. Would only make him worse, in fact. He just hoped Waterford didn't run into either of the men he was looking for—not feeling as he did.

"Buy me a drink?"

The redhead was tall for a woman, a couple of inches less than six foot. Her fingers touched Hart's arm for a second, then pulled away. He faced her, looking at the smile that lived in the red mouth and died in the eyes. Her hennaed hair was in curls that looked brittle; as if they might snap off at a touch. Her shoulders and the tops of her breasts were white above the stained green of her dress.

"Buy me a drink?"

Hart fingered a coin from his pocket and flipped it down on to the counter. He called to the bartender. "Buy the lady a drink."

Setting his back to her he walked out of the saloon. A couple of riders moved slowly past. A man stepped around him on the sidewalk. In the sky the nearly perfect round of moon was sharpening. Across the square the lights in the bank were still shining, although its doors were locked. A couple of customers came out of the Beaumont Dry Goods and Suttlers store.

Hart stared through the half light at the figure moving along by the side of the bank. He hesitated a moment or two, nodded, and began to walk across the square.

The figure half turned towards him and hurried to the mount tied to the end of the hitching post.

"What's the hurry, Henry?"

The big, bearded man turned fully now, standing close by his horse. "Hart. What do you want?"

"What's your all-fired hurry?"

"Nothing special."

Hart moved in a little closer. "You seemed mighty anxious to get away,"

"From you? I didn't see you."

Hart smiled, not believing. "Been making a business call?" he asked, nodding in the direction of the bank.

"Why d'you ask?"

"Late for business, ain't it? The bank's all locked up."

"Crompton's still there. He knew I was coming in."

"Uh-huh." Hart looked up at the light which now showed from the upstairs window. "Minin' business, was it?"

Jake Henry started to answer, paused, then: "Yes. I'm heading back there right now."

Hart nodded and moved away. When the bearded man was in the saddle, Hart turned back. "You'd better keep your eyes open. Dan Waterford's round town."

"What's that to me?"

"He seems anxious to finish what he started the other night."

Henry wheeled his horse around.

"Without you to protect him, he doesn't stand a chance."

Hart watched as the mine manager flicked the reins and set his mount into a trot. When horse and rider were out of sight, he went back into the Silver Star and bought himself a bottle of whisky. If anything happened he'd hear soon enough. What he wanted right then was a little of his own company, a little whisky bright and warm at the back of his throat, maybe even a few memories that didn't carry their sting in the tail.

Two thirds of the way up the stairs something stopped him. Nothing he could pin down, but something that made the hair on the back of his hands lift and crackle, which sent a cold scoop of air around his stomach, which dried the inside of his mouth.

He flicked the safety loop from the hammer of his Colt and trod softly up the remaining stairs, waiting outside the door.

10

SOUND of someone whistling along the street outside, further back a horse neighing restlessly, from downstairs the noise of pans being used in the kitchen. Hart worked to close those from his mind, concentrated on the room before him, on the far side of the door.

He thought he heard a slight movement, like the weight of a man shifting balance in a chair, possibly the rub of material as one trouser leg was crossed over another. Breathing? Hart could not distinguish it from his own. Outside the whistling stopped abruptly. Hart's fingers found the mother-of-pearl grip of his Colt .45, tightened round it, drew it smoothly up from the holster.

A pan clanked against the stove.

Hart set his left hand on the round, brass doorhandle and held his breath, face muscles taut, body leaning backwards. He turned the handle and threw the door back, going in fast, gun raised, swivelling to cover the entire room in a fast arc.

Lacy was sitting in the one comfortable chair, the lamp lit on the bedside table behind him, so that his face was in shadow. All Hart could distinguish was an oval paleness, the metallic glint from one corner of his spectacle frames. One suited leg folded over the other, right over left. The vest of his grey suit buttoned through neatly.

Hart stared at him, keeping the Colt steady. The door was open wide behind.

"I thought we might talk." Lacy's voice was clipped, precise.

Hart continued to stare, features of Lacy's face taking shape gradually.

"Without being disturbed."

Hart stepped back into the doorway and bent down, scooping up the bottle of whisky and then pushing the door shut with his boot. He gave Lacy a quick glance, slipped the Colt back down into its holster and pulled at the top of the bottle.

There were a couple of glasses on the chest of drawers. He poured whisky into both of them and handed one to Lacy, who nodded thanks and took it, perching the glass on his knee and making no move to drink.

Hart took a swallow and wiped the back of his hand over his mouth. "What d'you want to talk about?"

"You."

"Go on."

"There were things you didn't tell me. Things you held back."

"Yeah."

"You didn't say anything about killing Carter and the others."

"I told you. I deal with the man who pays me."

"And I told you—Mr. Beaumont doesn't concern himself with such things. He pays me to handle them for him."

Hart moved towards the window and glanced out; three riders were heading slowly towards the square, coat collars pulled up.

"He seemed interested enough."

Lacy blinked behind his spectacles, once.

Hart drank some more of the whisky. "Anythin' else?"

"Jake Henry."

"What about him?"

"You've been riding him hard. He doesn't like it—makes him nervous." Lacy uncrossed his legs. "D'you have any reason for wanting to do that?"

Hart thought a few moments. "A lot of silver's bein' lost . . . one way or another."

"And you think Henry's behind it?"

Hart looked at him evenly. "I think someone is."

Lacy coughed into the back of his hand, a sharp, dry cough. "You have any proof?"

"I ain't accusin' no one. Not yet."

Lacy stood up, the glass of whisky in his left hand. "When you do, come to me first."

Hart moved away from the window. "Lacy, for a clever man you're awful slow at pickin' some things up. If I need to talk to anyone it'll be to Beaumont, direct."

Lacy put down the glass, whisky untouched, "And you know what I've said before. I run those kind of things for Mr. Beaumont. Now is that clear?"

Hart shook his head. "It's clear but I'll tell you, you ain't runnin' me."

Lacy's face tightened. "We'll see."

He was in the doorway when the sound of an explosion shook the room. Hart whipped round, throwing open the window. Whatever had happened, the noise had come from the square. Lacy glanced at Hart and then turned fast, hurrying down the stairs. Hart picked up the Remington, breaking the barrels as he ran and checking the load. He passed Lacy inside the boarding-house door, pushing past him and out into the street.

Men were running in the direction of the square and Hart raced between them, the sharp crack of pistol fire ahead of him. As he neared the centre of the noise he slowed, crossing on to the boardwalk.

A rider turned into the street, bending

low over his saddle, boots kicking, his arm rising and falling as he lashed the horse into a gallop. Hart steadied himself, turning and drawing his Colt as he swung round to follow the speed of the man's escape. He squeezed back on the trigger, trying to ignore the blurred shapes of men that moved across his vision.

The single report cut clear through the air and for a few seconds horse and rider continued on their way. Then the whipping arm flailed wildly, boots slipped from the stirrups and the man toppled to the ground, bouncing heavily, rolling, then still.

From the corner of his eye Hart noticed that Lacy had caught up with him and was standing close by the storefront.

He ignored him and carried on into the square. The side wall of the bank had been blown out into the alley alongside. Two men on horseback churned the ground in front of the bank, three other animals milling around close by. The front windows of the bank had been shattered by the blast and now men were kneeling behind them, firing out. Pistol shots came back at them from the Silver Star opposite and from one of the first floor windows in the assay office.

People stood at the entrances to the square, watching the shooting, waiting to see what the regulator would do. His first decision was made for him. Someone ran through the bank door and hurled a sack up to one of the mounted men, ducking under the hitching rail and trying to grab at the dangling reins of one of the free horses.

Hart ran diagonally, making sure he didn't give his back to whoever was snapping off shots from the saloon. The Colt was still in his right hand and he brought it up fast, snapping off two shots. The first cut through the air close by the head of the rider who'd grabbed the sack, the second screamed along the boardwalk and made the man who'd come from the bank scuttle back towards the doorway.

Both mounted men wheeled their horses round, trying to control their fear.

"Hold it!" Hart's voice struggled to rise

above the clamour. The two men turned their horses and drove them towards the far side of the square. Hart jumped out towards them, slipping the Colt back into his holster and bringing up the shotgun. He saw one startled face, a mouth which opened wide and eyes that stared down. He steadied the shotgun with his right hand and fired.

The face disappeared. The man's body was smashed back from the saddle, lifted into the air and suspended while the horse galloped on. While he was still falling, Hart turned fast, drawing the shotgun away and diving his hand back towards his Colt.

It wasn't necessary. A volley of shots from the doorway of the saloon rocked the second rider in the saddle. Slugs shook him like a rat in the mouth of an angry dog. Chest and arms leaked blood.

In the middle of the square the man Hart had blown from his horse was slowly, painfully trying to crawl. His arms were crooked out in front of him, fingers bent and seeking purchase in the mud-packed ground. He lifted his head as if to see but he could see nothing. His eyes, his face, no more than a shredded pulp above his lacerated body.

"What's goin' on?"

Hart ducked down behind the double doors, lifting his Colt and reloading. He recognized the squat figure of the banker behind a table he'd overturned for cover, a couple of other men he knew by sight —all three with pistols drawn.

"I was in here taking a drink," said the banker. "Next thing I knew there was this explosion and when I got to the door here half the bank wall had been blown away."

One of the men angled himself tight against the wall beside the doors and fired across the square. An answering shot skimmed through the space above his head and ended up in the plaster of the far wall.

"One man was outside holding a bunch of horses. It was obvious what was going on. I pulled my gun and Ben and Roy chimed in."

"Yeah, we sure put paid to one of 'em," laughed the man by the door. "He rode this way an' we took him down out of his saddle like it was a Sunday shoot."

"You got no idea who they are?" Hart asked.

The banker shook his head. "Sorry. All I seen is what you can see from here. One thing, though, weren't no one hangin' round when I closed up. Whoever it was must've ridden in and got on with it straight off."

Hart nodded. "Like they knew exactly what they was goin' to be doin'."

A couple more shots came from the bank and the two men now at the doors gave answering fire.

Hart moved away from the table. "This could go on half the night," he said. "Let's talk 'em out of there."

He stood beside the left side of the doors and cupped his hand to his mouth. "You over there in the bank. There ain't no way you're gettin' out alive. Throw out your weapons an' walk clear."

For several moments there was no reply

and Hart thought he was going to have to try a second time. Then: "There's only me an' one other feller. He's wounded pretty bad." A pause followed in which it was possible to hear the low moanings of one of the men lying out in the square. "How do we know we can trust you? How do we know you won't cut us down as soon as we come out?"

"You got my word."

"Who are you?"

"I'm the regulator here. Now toss out your guns and step out with your hands high."

Hart stepped back from the doorway a little. The banker looked up at him with his round face shiny with sweat. "You don't trust them do you?"

Hart shrugged. "Maybe. Much as I'd trust anyone."

He cupped his hand to his mouth again. "You folk out there, you make sure you keep your guns up when they come out. Don't interfere now."

Again a moan of pain from the square. The man whom Hart had shotgunned out of his saddle was still trying to crawl, blindly, painfully across the ground.

"There's someone movin'," called one of the men at the opposite side of the door.

"Okay."

Hart watched as first a rifle, then a pair of pistols were thrown out on to the sidewalk in front of the bank. He paused then stepped outside, Colt drawn and raised. There was a scattering of people down at the end of the saloon, pushing back into the alley. More men were over by the dry goods store. Whoever had been firing from the upstairs window of the assay office had put out the light and lowered the blind.

"Come on out with your hands high."

They came through the broken door slowly, one man leaning heavily against the other, dragging his leg behind and grasping the other round the neck. They moved off the boards and on to the square, coming cautiously forward. Hart went to meet them.

He could see that both men were

wounded. The one who was walking straight looked to have been hit in his right arm; the other had a shattered leg which jerked pain through him with every fresh movement. Their faces came out of the shadow and Hart knew that he'd not seen either of them before. Some of the townsfolk began to follow him out into the square, moving behind him on his right.

Hart stood his ground and dropped the Colt back down into its holster. The gunned man had ceased moving, ceased moaning. One of the bank robbers was lean, stubbled, his nose razored down his face; the second, crippled one was younger despite his face, contorted as it was with spasms of pain.

Someone came close up on Hart's right and he glanced round, seeing that it was Lacy. As his vision shifted he realized the lean man was pushing his hand towards his coat pocket. Hart swung his head back, hand covering his Colt, making sure. Before he could be certain what was happening, two shots sounded close behind. The lean man jumped backwards as if he'd been hit, surprise flooding his stubbled face. He jerked away from the second man, who fell sideways to the ground, shot again himself, a fresh wound high in his chest.

Hart stared at Lacy, standing composed, Smith and Wesson .38 still in his hand, still levelled forward.

Hart's fingers grazed the mother-of-pearl on his gun grip. "What the hell was that for, Lacy?"

Lacy looked at him mildly. "He was pulling a gun. You were looking round at me. There wasn't anything else to do."

"I told everyone to keep out of this. It was my play."

Lacy nodded. "And you were going to lose."

Hart turned away. A crowd was beginning to circle the dead men. The banker paused, then hurried past, heading back to see exactly what had happened.

"You sure it was a gun he was reachin' for?" Hart asked over his shoulder.

Lacy shrugged. "See for yourself."

The stubbled face stared up at the evening sky blankly. A splash of blood smeared his lips and the end of his sharp nose. Lacy's slug had taken him inches above the heart. He had keeled over backwards, legs folded underneath him, arms spread wide.

Hart looked at the wound and considered—Lacy had drawn and fired accurately as fast as any man he'd ever seen. It was something worth thinking about.

He bent down and reached into the dead man's coat pocket. His fingers closed around the metal of a small pistol; he lifted it clear and turned slowly, tossing it down on to the ground in front of where Lacy was standing.

"Looks like you was right," he said grudgingly.

"Looks as if you might owe me an apology. Or at least your thanks."

Hart stared at him a moment longer then turned on his heels and walked over to the bank. The banker was standing in the midst of a pile of rubble and torn and crumpled papers, carefully counting dollar bills into neat piles. Coins littered the floor. A dark green metal safe was on its side by what remained of a partition wall. Hart could see that the rear of the safe had been blown away.

Hart looked down at the banker's balding head, pink skin glowing in the light of the kerosene lamp he'd lit and stood nearby.

"They get away with anything?"

The banker finished counting a pile of bills before answering. "It's impossible to tell exactly. But I . . . I mean how could they? Didn't we stop them all from getting away?"

Hart shrugged quickly. "Maybe. Only we don't know for sure how many of them there were."

The banker looked up at him, blinked and wiped the edge of his hand down the side of his face.

"Were you holding a lot of money?"

The banker nodded. "Oh, yes. Yes. A great deal. You see—"

"Jake Henry was in here earlier this evenin', wasn't he?"

"Ye . . . yes. Why?"

"Sort of late."

"Well . . ."

"I mean, after normal business hours."

"Yes, but . . ."

"Was that usual?"

The banker wiped at his face again, sweat coming from his pores easily. His small eyes blinked inside his round face. "Sometimes. If Mr. Henry needed to make a special payment. A large sum of money, from a silver shipment, say, he'd come after banking hours. So as not to draw attention to the size of the sum he was depositing."

Hart nodded, a smile playing at the edges of his mouth. "Then no one'd know Henry made one of these special deposits this evenin'—no one except you an' him?"

The banker jolted backwards as if someone had poked him in the stomach hard.

"No more'n an hour before the bank

was raided." Hart fixed the banker with a stare. "Raided by a gang who just happened to know the way the safe was backed up against that side wall there."

"Look! I mean . . . what . . . what are you suggesting?"

The banker looked at Hart and then away; he rubbed his hands together, fingers intertwining, separating, locking. In the square behind men were carrying away the bodies.

"I've worked for Mr. Beaumont since the bank opened and in all that time there's never been a single complaint. Never one suggestion that there was anything, er, anything reproachful in the way I conducted the business."

Hart nodded. "How much Beaumont pay you for all this good service?"

The banker looked at him puzzled. "Two hundred dollars a month."

"Uh-huh. Maybe you got to thinkin' a couple of hundred dollars weren't enough for all that honest work."

"No, I . . ." Between his lips, the

banker's tongue was pale pink, flickering spittle.

"Or maybe someone suggested it to you. Someone in a position to use a little pressure."

"No!" It was a shout of defiance—the kind that a man made in spite of everything when he could see the ground crumbling away from under his feet.

The pink, sweating face stared up at Hart, eyes blinking fast. "No!"

Hart turned away, leaving the man there in the midst of the wreckage of his bank, leaving him there shaking, crying.

11

THE squirrel wrinkled its nose up at horse and rider. The copper-coloured head inclined to one side. Hart looked at the broad black-and-white stripe along the animal's side, it's stomach moving gently in and out. He clicked his tongue at the dapple grey and the squirrel turned and raced for the safety of the nearest pine, scrabbling quickly up the trunk and disappearing from sight along one of the branches.

The pine was succeeded by another and another, tapering steeply down the side of the canyon. Green scrub marked the far side of the canyon wall. Two thirds of the way down, the ground had been levelled out and a log cabin built, the ends of the logs jutting out and overlapping, the roof a low-angled V. Thirty or so feet below the cabin a mine entrance had been shored up. Another unsuccessful attempt to reap as much silver as the Beaumont mine.

Hart had been out to the Beaumont mine earlier, looking for Jake Henry, but no one had seen him since the previous afternoon. It seemed likely that, despite what he'd claimed, he hadn't returned there after depositing the money in the bank.

Hart had checked the Beaumont place too, but Lacy had denied seeing him and when he'd asked to talk to Beaumont the message had come back that Mason Beaumont wasn't admitting any visitors no matter what their business. Hart had ridden back along the avenue of trees, leaving Lacy on the porch, smart and smug.

He'd thought about riding on to see Dan Waterford, but after their last meeting in town there didn't seem to be a lot of point. Instead he'd come higher into the hills, just riding and thinking, mostly letting the grey choose her own path.

Now as he stared down at the cabin

something beyond it caught his eye. The peak was sheer in places, the rock weathered and flaking, reddish brown and bare. A sudden flash of silver, it could have been the rump of a deer, a bird's wing, the reflection of something metallic, a rifle.

Hart dismounted and led the horse along the narrow trail towards the cabin, keeping the animal between himself and whatever he'd seen on the mountain. Presuming it was still there.

He kept his eye on the rock ahead but there was no further sign of anything moving. Whatever it had been was apparently there no longer.

He considered turning back and riding around the canyon rim but since he was so far down towards the deserted mine he decided to continue. As the path angled round he could see a little of the far side of the cabin, the end of a wagon poking out.

Something triggered inside his head.

Once when he'd been riding for John Chisum down in Lincoln County he had come in on a cabin just the same. Not a sign of life, no smoke, no horses, not a single sign. Billy Bonney and Dick Brewer had been riding at the head of the bunch and Billy had been all for riding straight in, but Dick had held them back. There was a flat-bed wagon alongside the cabin, nothing loaded on it, just sitting there in the Pecos sun.

"What the hell!" Billy had ranted. "It's no more'n a fuckin' wagon!"

"That's right," Dick had agreed. "And a wagon's somethin' you can move. Cabin you can't. Man brings things in on a wagon an' if he leaves he takes it with him. Less'n it's bust up an' that one ain't."

Dick Brewer had pulled his rifle from the saddle scabbard and worked the lever. "That wagon's fine. It just might mean whoever brung it's still around."

Billy had spat at the ground and cursed some more but he'd done it Dick's way anyhow. They'd split up and moved in real careful. As it was one of them had to make the first move across the open space and that was a greaser named Angelo. He made five yards before a slug from a Henry took his right eye clean out. He was the only one Dolan's men did get though—at least, that day.

Hart pulled the mare to a halt and reached up for his own rifle. He wondered what had happened to Billy Bonney. He'd been wondering ever since he'd walked out on him and ridden out of New Mexico and into Indian Territory; had been wondering ever since Billy had sent two men after him and he'd had no choice but to draw on them and leave one for dead.

He looped the ends of the reins around a piece of dark green scrub and started to move down the sloping path.

Rifle in his left hand, he flicked the loop from the hammer of his Colt. The cabin was a hundred yards away now, no more. A bird hovered on the air stream above it, wings spread wide, head down, watching.

Suddenly the bird swooped and Hart stood quite still. After a few moments it rose into the air on the far side of the cabin and flew across the canyon, a small animal held tight in its claws.

Hart made the rest of the approach slowly, making as little noise as possible. He could see most of the wagon now and knew that it could be the same as one of those the group of trappers had ridden into Tago and out again.

Out again to where?

There was no reason for them to stay around, but . . .

He looked at the wagon and tried to remember, tried to be certain.

Hart sprinted the last twenty yards, stopping himself against the jutting ends of log at the angle between side and front wall. He listened and heard nothing other than his own breathing. Soft crunch of his own boots on the gravel strewn around the cabin. He tried to lift the latch on the door, but it was held fast by four nails driven deep into the timber.

Moving past the door, he pushed the rifle barrel against one of the wooden shutters at the window and it squeaked back.

Again, he waited, listening.

Heard, instead, the cry of Angelo as a rifle bullet drove through his head, splitting the eye socket; the insistent moaning of the bank robber he had shotgunned from the back of his horse in the town square. He set the rifle down, leaning it against the wall.

Hart leaped to the front of the window, both hands, clutching for the bottom of the frame and pulling himself up, vaulting through. As he landed in the musty shadow, his right hand sped to his holster and the Colt seemed to spring to meet it.

He swung through an arc, quick, then slow. Dust rose up from below him, separating and drifting back down. The sound of his boots echoed dully. The cabin was empty.

Hart pushed his tongue against the roof of his mouth: it was dry. He released the hammer of the Colt and let it fall back into the holster.

Outside again, he examined the wagon. It was in pretty fair condition and from the track marks around it had been moved recently, though not necessarily in the last couple of days. He tried to figure out if it was the same as the trappers had used, but there was no way of being certain.

He lifted his rifle away from the wall and moved back up the track to where he'd left his horse.

"Hey, Clay." He patted her warm neck as he freed the reins, turning her and slotting his left boot into the stirrup.

"Let's go."

The mare began moving as his weight lowered down on to her, right foot searching for the second stirrup. The crack of a rifle merged with a jolt that hammered into his body and he went backwards, clutching at air. One second he was almost mounted, the next the ground had come crashing to meet him and all of the breath was knocked out of his body. His head slammed against an outcrop of rock beside the track.

The grey shied and bolted yards up the path before she turned and looked back.

Hart lay still. His right leg was forked

from his body, the other straight out. One arm seemed somehow trapped behind his back; the fingers of the other stretched towards the place between chest and shoulder where the bullet had entered. Pain screeched through to his brain, sharp and raw. He fought to keep his eyes open but they were closing, closing, the lids like weights pressing down. He was breathing harshly through his mouth. His head was on fire.

There were so many things: he knew he had to keep awake, to move; he had to get to some cover; clear his own weapon from its holster and . . . had to . . . had . . .

Hart came awake slowly. Eyes closed, he struggled to remember where he was. Something solid pressed against his back and arms. He was sitting up, leaning. The crack of rifle fire jolted him and for a second he was uncertain if it was real or a memory. The jerk of pain across his chest assured him. He remembered falling from his horse, striking . . .

It was later, he had no way of knowing how long. He'd suddenly lost consciousness again and now he'd come round. Still the back of his head, his shoulder-blades rested on something solid and hard. His wound . . . he saw Kate Stein behind his closed eyes, walking towards him, bringing something for him. Her hair fell about her shoulders in long, dark tresses and she was wearing silver things like rings and . . .

His eyes were open and he was inside a bare cabin, bare now except for a bundle of things stacked in the far corner. A fire burned beneath the smokestack and a pan was set close by it. As Hart winced and tried to move away from the wall he'd been propped against, the door swung open.

"Hey!"

Dan Waterford stood with a bundle of logs in both arms, looking across at him.

"I was beginnin' to wonder if you were goin' to come round at all."

Hart blinked, turned his head. "How long . . . ?"

"Some hours."

Waterford lowered the logs down in front of the fire, throwing a few on to the back of the blaze and stacking the rest to one side.

"Mind you," he said, turning towards Hart, "I was glad enough you were out cold when I was cleanin' that wound of yours."

Hart looked down at the improvised bandage wound tightly about his left shoulder and his chest. His vest and shirt had been removed and the bandage strapped tight before the shirt had been draped back over his shoulders. The centre of the bandage was stained dark reddish-brown.

"You were lucky. The bullet went through without hitting a bone. Clean as a whistle. Almost. I boiled some water and dressed it best I could. It'll heal."

Hart looked puzzled. "But how come I was laid out for so long?"

Waterford pointed: "You hit your head on a chunk of rock. There's a lump there the size of a man's fist."

Hart tried to move, reaching up to feel the back of his head. The effort made him wince with pain.

"You'll not be moving too far for a few days."

Hart frowned. "We'll see."

Dan Waterford said nothing more for the moment. He pulled a muslin bag from the pile of things in the corner and took out a chunk of dried meat. He cut off a piece and handed it to Hart.

"When I was lookin' at that wound of yours, I noticed another one, recent, along your back."

Hart chewed slowly on the meat, nodded. "Yeah. I was lucky."

"Like today?"

Hart shrugged. "Maybe."

Waterford sat alongside the fire, resting on the wall. "Why d'you do it?"

"What?"

"Sell your gun."

Hart spat out a piece of gristle. "Maybe there isn't anything else to sell."

Waterford let it ride until he'd made coffee in the pan and poured both of them a mugful. "Then it means you keep movin' around, is that it?"

"Pretty much."

"Until someone gets luckier than you are."

Hart drank some of the coffee; it was too sour, too strong. He didn't answer.

"Don't you never want to settle down? Make a place of your own?"

Hart turned away and the movement sent a fresh stroke of pain lancing through him.

"Not ever?" Waterford persisted.

It had been a long time since Hart had thought about her, about Kathy. He'd almost convinced himself that he wasn't going to think about her again. Especially since he'd been spending time with Kate. But now: now there was nothing to prevent glimpses of her taunting his mind, his body. A picture of a face turning, hair falling against a bare shoulder, a yellow dress . . .

"Once," Hart said bitterly. "I thought about it once."

"And . . ."

But Hart wanted no more of it, no more conversation He set down the mug, most of the coffee remaining, leaned back on to the wall and closed his eyes. For a while he was undisturbed, then he heard Dan Waterford shifting around. After that he heard nothing.

A rattle on the cabin roof woke him and his hand went towards the pistol close by his side. Small movements like a bird. Inside the cabin it was dark, cracks of light starting to show from door and windows. At the other side of the fire, the form of Dan Waterford stirred, turned.

"What is it?"

"Nothin'."

Waterford threw off his blanket and sat up, wiping sleep from the corners of his eyes. He yawned and wiped at his eyes some more; got up and opened the door.

"It's past dawn."

"Yeah."

Hart was able to get up with the help of floor and wall. He gritted his teeth against the tight throbbing from the rifle wound and moved towards the door. Waterford was bringing water from the stream thirty yards below.

He touched the back of his head gingerly; the bump had gone down somewhat but the end of it was tender, the skin scabbed and broken. He tried to move his left arm but it was stiff at the shoulder and sore.

"It's goin' to take a few days, I told you."

"I don't have a few days."

"I don't see . . ."

"Somebody shot at me. Tried to kill me. Can't you understand that?"

Waterford stood his ground, stared at him. "Like you understood about my brothers?"

Hart started to reply, but shook his head instead. Neither of them spoke until they were eating stale cornbread and drinking coffee.

"How come you took me in? Looked after me?"

Waterford looked at him, a trace of a

smile in his brown eyes. "You know the story about the Good Samaritan?"

"Uh-uh."

Waterford looked away: "Just somethin' my ma taught me."

Hart chewed on the bread and swilled it down with the bitter coffee, trying all the while to forget the ache in his chest and shoulder.

"You got an idea who it was?" Waterford asked after a few moments.

"Could be it sets you an' I in line."

"How would that be?"

Hart told him about the raid on the bank and his suspicions concerning Jake Henry.

"Surely strange for him not to be at the mine. You don't think maybe he's run out?"

Hart shook his head. "If he's at what I think he is, then he'll stick as long as he can. There's too much money involved to throw it in if there are ways of gettin' round it."

"Like?"

"Like my hunch is that was Henry up

there with a rifle an' lookin' for me just like I was lookin' for him."

Waterford rubbed the faint stubble of his chin. "You're goin' after him then?"

Hart stood up, wincing despite himself. "I'd sure like to find him. Ask one or two questions he might not want to answer."

He reached for his gunbelt, biting the flesh inside his lower lip to prevent himself from calling out. Thoughtfully, he buckled on the belt and bent to tie the thin leather thong at the inside of his leg. Yes, he wanted to ask Jake Henry a couple of questions at least.

12

"YOU going to take all night about it?"

"Shut up!"

"I only—"

"I said, shut up!"

The red-head pouted and sat higher up in the bed, pulling the sheet up over her breasts; she absent-mindedly combed a hand through one side of her curled hair and shivered with a cold that was inside her only.

Jake Henry sat on the side of her bed, head bent forwards, shirt opened to the waist and spreading over his hips and on to the sheet. His pants and coat were folded over a chair that stood by the window; a pair of long johns lay in a heap on the floor by the chair legs. His boots stood alongside the chair.

Henry wiped his hand over his bearded face and lurched up from the bed, making it rock. He fumbled in the pockets of his coat and finally came out with the silver flask. He slumped back on to the bed and unscrewed the top.

The woman made a noise, not a word, just a noise that was midway between resignation and disgust.

"What the hell's the matter with you?"

"Nothing."

"Then what was that row about?"

"It doesn't matter. Just let's . . . let's get on with it. I could be earning money."

Henry pulled the flask away from his mouth, brandy spilling down his chest. He leaned towards her and threw a punch that never came near her face.

"You fuckin' whore! You're getting money. I already paid more'n your worth twice over."

She glared back at him, back pressed hard against the bedhead. "You paid me all right and you've already taken more than your time."

"To hell with that!"

Henry stood up and took another swallow at the flask, the brandy singing through his brain, warming the back of his throat.

"You'll take what's coming to you!"

The red-head turned her face aside and laughed—a harsh brittle laugh that made Jake Henry's temper flare again. He jumped across the bed at her, the flask falling from his hand and bouncing from bed to floor. His right hand grabbed at her wrist, missed, caught her arm. She struggled away, lifting her legs from the sheet and letting fly.

Henry grunted as one of her feet landed in his stomach and a flailing hand hit him on the side of his face. He rocked sideways off the bed, catching hold of the sheet and taking it down with him.

Naked, the woman ran for the door. Her hand was on the handle when Henry flung his arm round her neck and dragged her back into the room. He spun her round and shook his head; slapped her face twice at close range, his thick fingers going back and forth, jerking her head from side to side.

"Christ, you . . . !"

Henry got hold of her shoulders and forced her back towards the bed.

"Don't you think . . ."

He threw her down and as she bounced from the mattress he jumped on top of her, knee driving hard down into her thigh. She screamed and scratched and tried to bite his arm, her mouth snapping tight shut with scrapings of skin between her teeth.

Henry rammed his elbow down against her breast and she jerked to one side, certain that she was about to vomit.

She didn't.

Henry prised her legs wider apart with his knees and pushed himself inside her: even then it was difficult.

She lay there, blood running from her nose, one side of her mouth, trying to think of anything other than what was happening. Sweat slid from Henry's body on to her own, his weight rocked heavily against her, arms pressing her down. Muffled groans came from his open mouth; eyes closed tight; breath harsh through his nostrils.

"Come on," she said inside her head. "Come on, you useless bastard. Finish it! Finish! Finish!"

The last two words sounded out loud and he moved his face aside and stared into her eyes and there was no mistaking the loathing and shame that lived inside him.

He thrust deep again and again but nothing could prevent the strength slipping away from his body, the beginnings of humiliation. Again and again.

The door opened so quietly that he failed to hear it. It closed the same way. The woman gazed over Jake Henry's shoulder at the man in the half-light. Her eyes widened and her mouth began to open into a shout of warning.

Hart raised his hand towards her and she let her mouth close soundlessly.

He drew the Colt and moved closer to the bed, stepping softly. When he was near enough, he pressed the end of the barrel into the centre of Henry's back.

Jake Henry jerked sideways, a wordless

shout cutting short as he saw Hart standing over him, the pistol in his hand.

"Get up."

Henry pulled away from the woman's legs and she drew her knees up tight in front of her chest.

"Get up an' over there!"

Mouth open, Henry scrambled away from the bed. He began to stretch for his clothes but a word from Hart stopped him.

"The wall. Flat against the wall."

Hart glanced at the red-head. "Are you okay?"

She nodded, scarcely moving her head.

"Get dressed and get out."

She slid from the bed and hurried to the wardrobe. Hart ignored her, concentrating on the frightened man before him.

"Okay, I'll tell you why you're so damned surprised. It's 'cause you thought the only time you'd see me again was when someone came on my body up by that abandoned mine and brought it back down into town."

"No, I . . . that ain't true . . . I don't know what you're talkin' about."

The woman let herself out of the room, leaving the door on the jar. Hart backed towards it and kicked it shut with his boot.

Henry was figuring his chances of getting to the gun that was in his holster, the gunbelt hanging from the end post of the bed. Hart saw his glance and smiled.

"Why don't you? I'll put a slug in that spreading gut of yours that'll leave you alive long enough to tell me what I want to know an' then you'll die in a lot of pain. Slow pain."

Jake Henry shivered. "Can I . . . my clothes . . ."

"That can wait."

The sweat was drying on his body, cold and clammy.

"It was you, wasn't it?"

Henry shook his head; Hart brought up the Colt until it was level with the bearded man's face. He held his arm straight and began, slowly, to squeeze back on the trigger.

"Oh, God, yes! All . . . all right, yes."

"And the bank?"

Henry twitched, his eyes blinking fast. "You an' the banker, you set it up between you. With me around fixin' to rob the silver shipments wasn't goin' to be so easy, so you thought you'd get the money another way. Just for a change. Anythin' so long as you could keep your fingers dippin' into that pile of money that Mason Beaumont reckons is his."

Jake Henry stared back at him, saying nothing; his lower lip hung down and his arms and legs were trembling.

"Funny thing, while he sits in that fine house of his tryin' to pretend the South's risen again out here, there's folk takin' him for every cent they can."

Henry turned his head a little, guttural sounds coming from his throat. He coughed into the palm of his hand. "What do you care? What does it matter to you what happens to Beaumont's money?"

"It matters because he's payin' me for it to matter."

Henry moved a few inches away from

the wall. "We'll pay you more. Whatever you're gettin' we'll double it, treble it. Anythin' you want." His dark eyes looked at Hart with a vestige of hope. "What d'you say?"

"I say you're steeped in shit!"

Jake Henry flushed red and he moved towards the edge of the bed, fists held down by his sides and bunched. "Who the hell are you to talk to me like that? You're nothin' but a hired gun. A nothin'."

"That's right," Hart sneered. "An' you're a somethin' who'll murder and rob to get what he wants."

Henry raised his fist. "It's easy for you to shelter behind that gun of yours an' say that. If you—"

Hart released the hammer on the Colt and slid it down into the holster. He untied the thong at his thigh and slipped the end of the belt through the buckle, laying the gunbelt on the bed.

"Okay, Henry, now I don't have nothin' special keepin' you back an' I'll say it again. You're a liar an' a thief an' a murderer. Now what you goin' to do about it?"

Jake Henry moved around the end of the bed, fists up in front of his chest. He got to within four feet of where Hart was standing and swung a wild punch at Hart's head. Hart pulled his face back and let the fist sail wide. He changed position and crouched waiting for the next two blows, which he evaded just as easily. Henry waited, breathing heavily through his mouth, moving round Hart and looking for an opening. He thrust out his left hand, palm open, and ducked in underneath it, head aiming for Hart's chest.

Hart side stepped and brought the flat of his right hand down on to Henry's neck.

The big man rocked to the wall, crashing against it and cannoning away, almost losing his balance. Hart let him have time to recover before punching him three times—once in the stomach to double him forward, then twice in the face. Blood spurted from Henry's nose, spotting the sheet, the floor boards. Henry shook his head to clear it and more blood speckled the room.

Hart waited again and this time he hit the mine manager on the point of the jaw and the man went back on his heels, tottering. Hart went in quickly, following up with a couple of quick blows to the body.

Henry struck the door and swayed forwards, head hanging down, blood and mucus dripping towards the floor.

"Right, now you can tell me the rest. What I really want to know."

Henry shook his head slowly, as if he hadn't heard Hart properly; as if he didn't want to hear him, didn't want to understand.

Hart moved closer: "Who else, Henry? Who else is in on it with you?"

The bloodied face stared at him, eyes glazed.

"Who?"

Henry began to shake his head, to look away. Hart took hold of him by his bare shoulders and shook him like a bundle of clothes. Then he slammed him back against the door so viciously that the impact cracked one of the panels of wood.

"All right, you crooked bastard, we'll do it the hard way."

He reached inside his shirt and drew the knife from inside the Apache sheath which hung from his neck.

Henry stared at the blade in spite of himself; images formed behind his eyes and no matter how hard he tried to shake them clear he could not. He had known fear in his life before but never like this.

The fear made him rock back against the sides of the door and propel his body forward, straight for Hart, oblivious of the knife now, solely intent upon reaching the gun on the bed. Hart, surprised, pulled the knife aside, jutting out his leg to trip the man as he charged. Henry stumbled to the left, his hand still straining for the Colt in the holster. His left arm banged into the bedpost, his right hand touched the leather of the belt and pulled it inches towards him.

Hart slashed down with the knife and

the point sheered through skin and flesh midway down the forearm. Henry dropped the gunbelt as though it were burning; his arm was burning. For a second he stared at the bright spray of blood against his dark skin, bubbles that sprang out then joined in a line.

Hart caught hold of him by the scruff of his neck and, heavy as Henry was, hurled him once more against the door.

"All right, you bastard, that was your chance!"

"No! No! I'll tell you. For Christ's sake I'll tell—"

The shots came close together, ripping through the wood of the door. The second shot sent the door smashing into Henry's back as his body was kicked forward into Hart's arms. One slug exited through his neck, deflecting upwards from his ribs, the other wedged itself alongside the spine.

Hart held the shot man for seconds, taken off guard, numbed. Shouts sounded from below. Hart pushed Jake Henry aside on to the bed and jumped through the door drawing his gun as he did so.

Men were standing by the bar and beside tables, staring at the stairs, at the swinging bat-wing doors. Hart took the steps three at a time and as his feet touched the boards of the saloon floor, two more shots rang out in the street outside.

He ran towards the sound, arriving at the door in time to hear the noise of a horse being driven off at a gallop. A body writhed in front of him, half on the boardwalk, half in the street. Hart knew that it was Dan Waterford.

He stepped past him, untying the grey's reins from the hitching post and stooping underneath, ready to mount. He got as far as gripping the saddle pommel and lifting his boot towards the stirrup—then he pulled the horse back round and looped the rein around the post once more.

There were several men bending about Waterford's body and Hart pushed through them, kneeling down and turning Waterford's face carefully towards him.

"Anyone sent for the doctor?"

Mumbles of no.

"Then get movin' an' do it!"

The bystanders glanced at one another before one of them hurried away.

Waterford's eyes opened for an instant, flickered, closed. Hart opened the wounded man's vest and saw the darkly spreading stain covering the left side of his chest. He wondered if he should move him and thought not. Instead he told someone to fetch a lantern.

In the yellow-orange light Waterford's face looked younger, paler. A thin trail of blood ran from the corner of his mouth on to his chin, and then curled on to his neck. His eyes were still closed. Hart was listening to the weak beat of his heart, head against his chest, when the doctor arrived.

A short, stubby man with bushy eyebrows and thin, fine hands, he knelt opposite Hart and opened his black bag.

He looked at Hart for a moment, then felt Waterford's pulse, frowning as he did so.

"Can we move him?"

The doctor shook his head. "No point."

Hart looked at him.

"After." The doctor leaned up and laid Waterford's hand across his body. As he did so, a spasm shook the dying man and his head thrashed from side to side until Hart caught it between his hands.

Dan Waterford opened his eyes and this time they stayed open.

"La . . . Lacy . . . it was . . ."

The voice was little more than a gargling whisper and Hart had to bend low to hear it; speckles of blood burst from the bubbles on Waterford's lips and broke against the side of Hart's face. Instinctively, he wiped them away.

"Lacy . . . I . . . tried . . ."

"I know."

Waterford's eyes closed and his head jerked back against the sidewalk. Hart glanced across at the doctor, who was refastening his bag.

"Can you hear what I'm saying?" Hart asked.

There was no response and he repeated the question. This time Waterford nodded, eyes still shut.

"Henry's already dead. I'll get Lacy. You don't worry. I'll get him. For everythin'. For . . . this."

Dan Waterford gave no sign of having heard. He was no longer in Tago, no longer stretched up on to the boardwalk, no longer suffering the agony of dying. He was standing on top of a heap of gravel in the Bowery, his face red with anger and pride as hordes of ragged urchins ran from his fury. His coat was torn and ripped, his body was bruised, his head blooded—but he was king. King of Gravel Mountain.

Hart looked down at the smile that spread slowly over Dan's face, the lips that parted and the blood that burbled out and ran down on to his shirt, joining the blood already thickly there.

He stood up and closed his own eyes for a moment, shaking his head. Then he nodded to the doctor. "See to him. There's a couple of graves up on the mountain, by the claim he worked. He's to be buried there."

Hart took a handful of coins from his pocket and handed them over. The red-head in the saloon doorway took a pace towards him and stopped.

"Thanks," began on her bruised lips and ended unsaid.

Hart looked at her and turned away.

13

THE fly circled the sleeping figure, endlessly buzzing. Occasionally, it darted in towards the round, white face, the slack, pale skin. Once it landed for several seconds on the purple lips and hung there, camouflaged.

Its restless movement seemed to fill the room, to dominate everything except the sweet, sickly smell which permeated all.

Mason Beaumont woke to it, one eye opening before the other, the lid lazily flapping back down. The round, violet bottle stood on the table beside the white leather chair, the glass next to it empty except for a small cloud of water at the bottom.

Suddenly the fly's buzzing stopped: Beaumont jerked awake, his right arm falling sideways away from the chair, curled, rounded fingers brushing against the pile of the carpet. Beaumont moved his back uneasily, the silk of his shirt sticking to his skin. He fumbled for the glass and set it to his lips. Finding it empty, he let it fall through his fingers on to chair arm, lap, floor.

It was dark outside: no light came through the narrow openings left in the shutters. The lamp overhead burned brightly. Charlie must have come stooping in and lit it, in and out again without a sound, without a word.

Beaumont leaned back again and set his head against the rim of the chair. He closed his eyes and tried to bring back sleep; tried to summon up the dream he'd been immersed in before he'd woken.

What had woken him?

The fly came from hiding, unsettled, and the circling, the sound recommenced. The dream returned. Beaumont and his father seated astride stallions whose manes shone and glistened in the brightness of the sunlight. The thrum of hoofs on the hard earth. Changing. The sun extinguished in a single second. Now his father rode at the head of a group of men, anger exciting their faces; their voices shrill with it. Shadows blurring the grass in the aromatic moonlight.

He was not with them, but watching.

Caught in the dream, his body shuddered.

His father took hold of his arm, pulling him, leading him and he did not want to go; he struggled, fought. His father's voice quietening his pleas: strength of the man's hand hard against his weak efforts; the stern, black-bearded face glowering down.

"Mason, it is your duty, sir!"

The boy swung lightly in the breeze, as lightly, almost, as a spray of magnolia. His face, the glistening, black skin, the tight curls of the head, all beautiful—except . . .

Except the way one side of the face was twisted up by the knot, big and clumsy at the side of the neck; strain of the rope against which the boy's body had bounced, swung, battled.

Mason Beaumont stared at the face, beautiful face, saw and remembered the same face smiling, laughing, playing close to himself, with himself.

His father took hold of his shoulders and led him sternly away. "A lesson," he heard the words over and over: "a lesson, a lesson."

Beaumont was awake again, without knowing it. Awake and looking at the portrait of his father on the wall, standing there in his military uniform, proud and ready to die for what he held most dear.

Beaumont almost laughed—he had died. For whatever reason, whatever code, he had died. Mason Beaumont leaned forward in the chair and grabbed at the bottle, catching it at the second attempt. He held it in front of his face, making it sway from side to side, side to side . . .

Set to his lips the bottle yielded nothing. His tongue tip pushed into the tiny neck of the bottle, tasting the final drops.

"Damnation!"

He whirled savagely in the chair and threw the bottle towards the door. It struck the wall and bounced sideways, rolling softly over the thick carpet and only stopping when it came to rest against Lacy's left boot.

Beaumont jumped, startled; he'd had no idea that Lacy was in the room. He didn't know how long he'd been there. He watched as Lacy bent down and retrieved the bottle and examined it.

Lacy was dressed in a grey suit with a thin stripe, his hair brushed neatly, his spectacles in place on his nose. He looked from the violet bottle towards Beaumont, then slowly carried it towards him, passing round behind the chair and setting it down on the table. He picked up the glass and put that alongside it.

Lacy stood in front of Mason Beaumont, looking down at him. Without knowing why, Beaumont felt nervous, afraid; he glanced away but all he could see was the eyes in the portrait staring at him. He pressed the palms of his hands against the sides of the chair and the sweat stuck them to the leather.

"Henry's dead." Lacy spoke so quietly,

calmly, Beaumont didn't think he'd heard him correctly. Then he realized that he had. But his head was muzzy and he had difficulty in concentrating.

"Why?" He wasn't certain if he thought the question only or said it.

"I killed him."

Something uncoiled deep in Beaumont's stomach. He wriggled his body inside his white suit, the white silk of his shirt. His mouth was dry, his purplish tongue moving soundlessly inside it like a swollen snake.

"You killed him?" The words came slowly, Beaumont's voice no longer high-pitched but lower, more hollow.

Lacy nodded, otherwise still.

"He . . . he was stealing from me wasn't he? It was him behind the robberies."

Again, Lacy nodded—the same economical, neat movement.

"I suspected it all along. That he was . . ." Beaumont hesitated, licking the edges of his mouth, levering his hands from the chair. "That was why you killed him? You found out what was going on."

A pause, the suggestion of a smile behind the spectacles, and then Lacy's head moved the other way, side to side, slowly.

Panic squirmed inside Beaumont. "Then I don't understand."

"I killed him because he was a coward. A coward." The word shuddered off Lacy's lips. "Despicable."

Beaumont's head rolled forward, eyes closed.

"But then you'd know all about that, wouldn't you, Beaumont? All about how despicable it is to be a coward."

Beaumont's head jerked forward, cheeks swelling, mouth opening, vomit rose to the back of his throat and he coughed, choking, as the bitterness filled his mouth and then slid back down. He didn't understand, didn't know why Lacy was talking to him the way that he was. Usually he was so respectful, now he wasn't even saying

Mr, just Beaumont, the name spat out as if it were something vile.

"What's it like, Beaumont? Spending all of your time inside this house, inside this room? Surrounding yourself with your own sweat, your own stench. How does that feel?"

Lacy's voice shouted the last word and he bent forward and took hold of Beaumont's shoulder, throwing him back against the chair.

"Well, Beaumont? How is it when you're terrified of daylight? Only able to get through a day or a night dosing yourself with this junk."

Lacy swept bottle and glass off the table with a swing of his arm. The crash shook Beaumont and his body leaned sideways from the chair; he closed his eyes tight, set his hands over his ears, waiting, waiting for it all to go away, to stop. Then he would be alone again; he could send for some more laudanum. He could rest in the warm dark of the room and . . .

Lacy moved to the wall and knocked a

number of framed daguerreotypes to the floor. He lifted the sabre and scabbard from its place and whirled it around so that the end of the weapon was pointing towards the chair.

Beaumont peered through lowered lids and slowly withdrew his hands from his face.

"Put . . . that was my father's sword . . . put it . . ."

Lacy flicked the weapon and the scabbard flew off, freeing the polished blade. The gold of the hilt turned about Lacy's hand, a knotted leather band looping downwards from it; the curve of the sabre glinted in the lamplight as Lacy turned it slowly, moving it in a sinuous circle that widened until it was the width of a man's head.

"What are you doing? Lacy, Lacy! I don't understand!"

The point of the sabre came to rest against Beaumont's temple, moving his head upright, forcing him to lean backwards again in the leather chair.

"No, you don't do you—you don't understand."

Lacy held the blade steady while he removed his spectacles, folding them one-handed and slipping them into his coat pocket. He took a pace backwards and raised his arm, taking the sabre above his head. Beaumont threw up an arm in front of his face and let out a choking scream of terror. Lacy whirled the blade through the air, sending it scything inches above Beaumont's head and then pivoting his whole body round and slashing the sabre end diagonally down the portrait of Beaumont's father.

Gasping, Beaumont lowered his arm and stared. A slice of canvas folded down, another was beginning slowly to curl upwards. The black-bearded face of Major Orville Beaumont disappeared from view.

Mason Beaumont levered himself up from the chair and stood in front of it; his head moved unsteadily, mechanically, jolting this way and that. His fingers opened and closed. His breath was thin and reedy. He lifted a hand and pointed at Lacy as if, in some way, he was no longer afraid.

Lacy watched him carefully, the sabre at his side. He knocked the pointing finger aside contemptuously.

"Lacy, I thought you were my friend." The voice was high, anguished, even though the fear had gone.

The tall, thin figure laughed in Mason Beaumont's face. "Beaumont, I despise you. I loathe and despise you and all you stand for. You brought your family money out here and built this house with it; you bought half that mountain back there and sent men to dig out a fortune in silver; you did all this while you were living underneath that picture of some cruel and stupid old man who was shot to pieces in the war. You stink away in this fetid room and give your orders and expect me to be your friend!"

Beaumont gulped the thick, sweet sourness of the air. "Then why did you pretend?"

Lacy laughed again. "Why? Why do

you think? Because as long as I could bleed you white it was worth the pretence, the games. As long as Henry did what I told him and didn't get out of line, things were fine. But then you had to send for this regulator and things weren't fine any longer."

The sabre began to lift towards Beaumont's body.

"Now things are changed."

The tip of the blade ran a line down the centre of the silk shirt.

"Now I want the keys to your safe." The blade nudged. "Quickly."

The sweat began to run again down Beaumont's face; it clogged the pits of his arms, his groin. He shook his head and the tip of the sword cut through the material of his shirt and traced a line through the pallor of his skin.

Beaumont shuddered, shook; he faltered forwards on to the sabre end and more blood was drawn before Lacy pulled it back.

"The safe."

"You can't . . ."

The stroke was swift and sudden: at first when Beaumont stared at his arm he thought all Lacy had done was to cut away the front of his jacket sleeve. Then he felt the quick pulse of burning pain and saw the skin begin to leak blood. He let out a moan of despair and through it Lacy heard the sound of a horse and rider approaching fast.

He cursed under his breath and hurried to the nearest window. Easing back the shutter he glimpsed in dim silhouette the tall figure on the dapple grey, slowing now as he moved between the lines of trees that led to the house.

Lacy frowned and let the shutter move back into place. He glanced quickly at Beaumont, who was kneeling now before the slashed portrait of his father, letting the blood from his cut arm drip endlessly down into the carpet.

He left the room, shutting the door behind him, checking as he went the Smith and Wesson holstered inside his coat.

Hart brought the grey down to a walk.

The porch was empty save for a wicker rocker; a lantern shone from above the entrance. Hart looked at the windows, seeing no movement. He slid down from the saddle and looped the reins about a post, stepping around the animal's rear. A sound at the side of the house warned him and his thumb flicked the safety thong away from the hammer of his Colt. Alert, he waited: the bent-backed Negro came cautiously around the corner.

"Sir, I don't know what's goin' on up there, but there's been such awful sounds."

"What sort of sounds?"

Before the servant could reply, something crashed loudly inside the house. Hart jumped up the steps and pushed the door open, going inside fast, hand covering the butt of his Colt.

In the hallway the flowers stood in vases, the same plethora of colours. Another crash sounded from the first floor. Hart ran up the stairs and along the corridor. He hesitated for a second outside the room in which he'd spoken to Beaumont before; glass and china crashed and splintered inside. He turned the handle and went in.

Mason Beaumont was close to the far wall, before a glass-fronted cabinet, the contents of which were strewn about the room. Hart's eyes quickly took in the spreading chaos. Chairs overturned, plates and cups shattered, glasses splintered; the only thing remaining on the wall behind Beaumont was the slashed portrait of his father.

Beaumont stared at Hart as if he failed to recognize him. A trail of saliva and vomit ran from the right side of his mouth; the sleeve of his coat on the left side was cut away and hung darkly, rich in blood. A dribble of blood came away from the curled fingers of Beaumont's left hand.

He threw back his head and let out a high, screaming laugh that was animal, inhuman. Hart felt something move inside himself that he didn't recognize. He went over to Beaumont and shouted at him, shook him; when that didn't work he took a pace backwards and slapped him hard around the face, twice.

The laugh stopped abruptly; Beaumont's head levelled and he saw Hart for the first time.

The Negro servant hurried past Hart and stopped beside his master, touching him carefully and leading him over towards the chair.

"You come over here now, sir. You sit down here. We'll look after you, we will."

The Negro looked up at Hart and there were tears in his eyes; he looked past Hart at the same time as Hart whirled about, hearing a footstep on the boards beyond the room.

The short-barrelled Smith and Wesson .38 was tight in Lacy's hand; everything about him was composed, calm. He looked at Hart through the round lenses of his wire-framed spectacles and moved slowly inside the room.

"You're stupid, Hart. You may be fast with that gun of yours, but you're stupid. Why else would you ride in here on your own and let a man come up behind you the way you've just done?"

Hart's eyes narrowed; his body began to dip into a crouch, fingers of his right hand arching out over the Colt. Lacy watched him, smiling tightly.

"That's it, Hart. Make your final stupid play. There'll be two bullets in you before your hand's closed around that grip."

Hart hesitated, knowing the truth of what Lacy had said. The pain from his left shoulder was driving through him, brought to life by his ride out from town.

Lacy took several more steps into the room; to his right, Mason Beaumont continued to moan in his chair, the Negro kneeling beside him.

"When you're dead, Hart," said Lacy, "I get it all. All."

Beaumont lurched forwards, nearly slipping from the chair. Lacy was distracted for a fraction of a second, but it wasn't enough. The gun didn't waver;

the finger remained tight against the trigger.

Beaumont was kneeling on the floor now, the Negro's arms cradling the top of his body. Pieces of his family's past littered the carpet all about him—the sabre lay to one side, a few feet to Beaumont's left.

Hart crouched slightly forwards, not taking his eyes off Lacy's face. "If it isn't me, it'll be somebody else, you know that don't you?"

"What are you talking about?"

"I'm sayin' you'll carry on grabbing what ain't yours until the day comes you try for too much. Maybe that time it won't be someone like him over there you're lyin' to, robbin' blind."

Hart nodded towards Beaumont, who was trying to stand now, the Negro helping him. With a cry he lost his balance and went heavily to the floor.

Lacy grinned, a tight smile passing across his tight-set lips.

"What I'm sayin'," Hart went on, goading him, "is that you're a doubledealin' bastard who needs to sneak up on a man from behind."

Lacy's smile froze on his face. "It doesn't pay to rile me, Hart. Not in your position. Not at all."

The Smith and Wesson came up a little, Lacy's arm straightening. The nerves in Hart's right hand tingled as the fingers hovered. Mason Beaumont struggled on the ground and the hilt of the sabre knocked against his hand: his eyes closed, widened, mouth opened in a shout; his fingers closed around the hilt and he swayed upwards, the Negro jerking unsteadily out of his way.

Lacy heard the movement and the cry —didn't want to turn—had to turn— head going round just as the figure in the white suit swung the sabre blade towards him.

Lacy jumped and pulled his pistol round towards Beaumont. Even as he fired the edge of the blade struck his side, the force of the blow cutting through his neat, striped suit, his shirt, cleaving between his ribs.

Hart drew as Lacy turned away, the Colt coming up from the greased holster, his thumb bringing back the hammer, the triple click lost in the midst of Beaumont's yell, Lacy's cry of realization as the sabre struck home.

Hart waited until Lacy staggered two, three paces back, surprise for the first time in his eyes. The Smith and Wesson was still in his hand and he fought to bring it level, pain washing over him.

Hart watched the gun come up, stared hard into Lacy's face and fired. The first shot split Lacy's breast bone and sent him back towards the door in a leap. His legs began to give under him and blood came easily now from the sabre wound in his side. Hart brought back the hammer a second time. He sighted along the barrel and fired. The bullet spun Lacy through a near circle, smashing through the ribs on the left side of his body and exiting between his shoulder-blades with a splatter of blood and tissue that clung to the wall beside the door.

Lacy was on all fours, crawling, trying

to crawl, not knowing where he was trying to go or why.

Beaumont watched him, fascinated, the sabre still in his right hand.

Lacy stared up at Hart, trying to focus his vision, desperate to shake clear the blurring which drifted in front of his eyes like clouds. Slowly, his fingers fumbled for his wire-framed spectacles, found them, lifted . . . they fell away from his grasp on to the carpet and Lacy's body convulsed twice, rapidly.

Hart stepped closer, left boot treading down on to the spectacles. Lacy heard as if in some clear distance the crunch and crackle of wire and glass, the clicking back of the hammer of a gun.

Nothing more.

From less than three feet, Hart put a slug into the top of Lacy's head and blew most of it away.

He continued to stare down at the dead man for several moments before stepping back and reholstering his gun. Mason Beaumont was swaying unsteadily, the servant hovering near him.

"Look after him," Hart said. "I guess I've done here."

As Wes Hart rode slowly along the avenue of trees he turned his head and looked back. A wash of light swept through the shutters of the upstairs room where Beaumont had lived. Flames licked at the woodwork; within a matter of moments thick smoke began to push up through the air towards a slim crescent of moon.

Hart clicked his tongue against the roof of his mouth and the grey broke into a trot. At the end of the avenue he reined her in and sat round in the saddle.

The top half of the house was ablaze. The pillars that stood alongside the porch were bright with flame. From where he was Hart could hear the crackle and fall; could smell the acrid, bitter smoke. Outlined against the fire, two figures moved haltingly across the porch, one supporting the other.

Hart turned away again: when he heard

the resounding crash that was likely the front wall caving in, he did not look back.

He was already thinking about other things; thinking that for too long he had turned away from too much. His left side and shoulder ached and he thought of Kate Stein and imagined the coolness of her hands on his body. When he'd picked up his things in Tago, that was where he would go.

Horse and rider rode the dark trail back to the silver town alone. Behind them, a shimmering red glow lit up the night sky as Beaumont's mansion burnt steadily to the ground.

Books by John B. Harvey
in the Linford Western Library:

HART: BLOOD ON THE BORDER
HART: TAGO

Other titles in the Linford Western Library:

FARGO: MASSACRE RIVER

by John Benteen

Fargo spurred his horse to the edge of the road. Its right hind hoof slipped perilously over the edge as he forced it around the wagon. Ahead he saw Jade Ching riding hard, bent low in her saddle. Fargo rammed home his spurs and drove his mount up to her. The ambushers up ahead had now blocked the road. Fargo's convoy was a jumble, a perfect target for the insurgents' weapons!

SUNDANCE: DEATH IN THE LAVA

by John Benteen

The land echoed with the thundering hoofs of Modoc ponies. In minutes they swooped down and captured the wagon train and its cargo of gold. But now the halfbreed they called Sundance was going after it, and he swore nothing would stand in his way—not Indian savagery of the vicious gunfighters of the town named Hell.

FARGO: THE SHARPSHOOTERS
by John Benteen

The Canfield clan, thirty strong, were raising hell in Texas. One of them had shot a Texas Ranger, and the Rangers had to bring in the killer. The last thing they wanted though was a feud. Fargo, arrested for gunrunning, was promised he could go free if he would walk into the Canfield's lair and bring out the killer. And Fargo was tough enough to hold his own against the whole clan.

SUNDANCE: OVERKILL
by John Benteen

Sundance's reputation as a fighting man had spread from Canada to Mexico, from the Mississippi to the Pacific. There was no job too tough for the halfbreed to handle. So when a wealthy banker's daughter was kidnapped by the Cheyenne, he offered Sundance $10,000 to rescue the girl. Sundance became a moving target for both the U.S. Cavalry and his own blood brothers.

FARGO: THE SHARPSHOOTERS

by John Benteen

The Canfield clan, thirty strong, were raising hell in Texas. One of them had shot a Texas Ranger, and the Rangers had to bring in the killer. The last thing they wanted though, was a feud. Fargo, arrested for gun-running, was promised he could go free if he would walk into the Canfields' lair and bring out the killer. And Fargo was tough enough to hold his own against the whole clan.

SUNDANCE: OVERKILL

by John Benteen

Sundance's reputation as a fighting man had spread from Canada to Mexico, from the Mississippi to the Pacific. There was no job too tough for the half-breed to handle. So when a wealthy banker's daughter was kidnapped by the Cheyenne, he offered Sundance $10,000 to rescue the girl. Sundance became a marked target for both the U.S. Cavalry and his own blood brothers.

DAY OF THE COMANCHEROS
by Steven C. Lawrence

Their very name struck terror into men's hearts—the Comancheros, a savage army of cutthroats who swept across Texas, leaving behind a bloodstained trail of robbery and murder. When Tom Slattery stumbled on some of their slaughtered victims, he found only one survivor, young Anna Peterson. With a cavalry escort, he set out to bring the murderers to justice.

SUNDANCE: SILENT ENEMY
by John Benteen

Both the Indians and the U.S. Cavalry were being victimized. A lone crazed Cheyenne was on a personal war path against both sides and neither brigades of bluecoats nor tribes of braves could end his reign of terror. They needed to pit one man against one crazed Indian. That man was Sundance.

GUNS OF FURY
by Ernest Haycox

Dane Starr, alias Dan Smith, wanted to close the door on his past and hang up his guns, but people wouldn't let him. Good men wanted him to settle their scores for them. Bad men thought they were faster and itched to prove it. Starr had to keep killing just to stay alive.

FARGO: PANAMA GOLD
by John Benteen

A soldier of fortune named Cleve Buckner was recruiting an army of killers, gunmen and deserters from all over Central America. With foreign money behind him, Buckner was going to destroy the Panama Canal before it could be completed. Fargo's job was to stop Buckner—and to eliminate him once and for all!

HELL RIDERS
by Steve Mensing

Outlaw Wade Walker's kid brother, Duane, was locked up in the Silver City jail facing a rope at dawn. When Wade rode into town the sheriff knew trouble had already begun. Wade was a ruthless outlaw, but he was smart, and he had vowed to have his brother out of jail before morning!

DESERT OF THE DAMNED
by Nelson Nye

The law was after him for the murder of a marshal—a murder he didn't commit. Breen was after him for revenge—and Breen wouldn't stop at anything . . . blackmail, a frameup . . . or murder. He was desperate now and vowed to find a way out—or make one.

HELL RIDERS
by Steve [illegible]

Outlaw Wade Walker's kid brother, Danny, was locked up at the Silver City jail for [illegible] a [illegible]. When Wade rode into town the sheriff knew trouble had already begun. Wade was a [illegible] outlaw, but he was smart, and he had vowed to [illegible] his brother out of jail before morning.

DESERT OF THE DAMNED
by Nelson Nye

The law was after him for the murder of a marshal—a murder he didn't commit. Breen was after him for revenge—and Breen wouldn't stop at anything ... blackmail, a frameup ... or murder! He was desperate now and vowed to find a way out—or make one.

LASSITER
by Jack Slade

Lassiter wasn't the kind of man to listen to reason. Cross him once and he'd hold a grudge for years to come—if he let you live that long. But he was no crueler than the men he had killed, and he had never killed a man who didn't need killing.

LAST STAGE TO GOMORRAH
by Barry Cord

Jeff Carter, tough ex-riverboat gambler, now had himself a horse ranch that kept him free from gunfights and card games. Until Sturvesant of Wells Fargo showed up. Jeff owed him a favour and Sturvesant wanted it paid up. All he had to do was to go to Gomorrah, a one-time boom town, and recover a quarter of a million dollars stolen from a stagecoach!